Twelve Months

Brittany Anne

Preface

Readers, please keep in mind this book is extremely fast-paced. Some chapters are longer than others, there's a reason for it. **This is not a cancer story.** This is the story of Addley's last year of life. Thank you for choosing this book, I hope you love Addley's story. This story contains talk of cancer, drowning, sibling death, mental health, death, and talk of suicide. Please do not read any further if such will upset you; your mental stability matters most to me.

This is for my brother in heaven who taught me that life is too short to not chase my dreams.

I'll love and miss you always

Die First – Nessa Barrett

Ghost of You - 5 Seconds of Summer

Wish I Had You – Ruel

Suffocate – Hayd

Falling Apart – Michael Shulte

Headlights – Alex Warren

Empty Room - Jamie Miller

Love Like This - Kodaline

Happiest Year – Jaymes Young

A Little Bit Yours – JP Saxe

Where the Shadow Ends(Acoustic) - BANNERS

Part of Me - Cian Ducrot

The Wisp Sings - Winter Aid

Call Your Mom - Noah Kahan

Long Live - Taylor Swift(Taylor's Version)

Even in the Dark - jxdn

Chapter One

June

Ever experienced that looming sensation that your life is on the brink of a significant change? No matter what I do, it lingers. My therapist labels it as anxiety, but I'm convinced it's more than that.

My world shifted when my grandfather passed away when I was ten. I initially felt relief until my parents broke the news after pulling me from school. At fourteen, my sister's tragic drowning at the beach, fueled by alcohol, left me breathless the night before.

Something feels awry now, but words escape me. Life appears fine, yet an unsettling intuition persists — a feeling that everything is on the verge of crumbling.

The ringing bell snaps me back to reality. Returning Mr. Martinez's textbook, I bid him farewell for the summer and headed to meet my boyfriend, Jameson.

We've been inseparable since freshman year, navigating high school together. Jameson, my breath of fresh air after Kenny's passing, my closest confidant.

"Finally! Junior year is over. One more year until it's just you and I at Stanford," Jameson cheers, sealing it with a cheek kiss.

"You and I against the world," I respond, sincerity in every word.

Our friends, Ellie, Matthew, and Robyn, join us. Each with a unique connection, shared history, and the promise of a memorable summer.

Amidst laughter and camaraderie, Mattie and Jameson's friendly clashes are a constant. Jameson suspects a hidden history, but we're just close friends.

As Ellie dashes home for her bag, I give Jameson a parting kiss, and Mattie and I hop into my jeep. Neighbors, I exchange rides for math tutoring, our friendship built on trust.

"So, when are you going to dump him?" Mattie bluntly questions, our routine conversation starting again. "I love him, Mattie. He loves me," I assert, defending my relationship.

As we pull into the driveway, playful banter ensues, ending in a water bottle prank. Apologizing, I rush inside, promising to meet them in the kitchen.

Between the weeks leading up to my parents' return, I spend quality time with Jameson and friends. We explore hidden trails, reminisce about high school, and indulge in late-night talks by the bonfire.

One sunny afternoon, we decide to embark on a spontaneous road trip, eager for the thrill of the open road. Our jeep becomes a vessel of adventure, carrying us through winding paths and scenic landscapes.

Stopping at a quaint roadside diner, we savor local delicacies, exchanging stories and laughter. The journey becomes a canvas for new memories, the miles unraveling tales of friendship and shared exploration.

As the sun sets, we find an idyllic spot by a lake, its waters reflecting the hues of the evening sky. We dip our toes in the cool water, sharing dreams and aspirations beneath the canvas of stars.

A weekend beach day becomes a highlight, filled with sandcastle competitions, beach volleyball matches, and the taste of salt in the air. Laughter harmonizes with the crashing waves, etching snapshots of joy into the album of our summer.

As the summer progresses, our conversations evolve into deep reflections on the future. Late-night talks become a space for sharing hopes, fears, and the intricate tapestry of our dreams.

One evening, Mattie opens up about his aspirations beyond high school, sparking a discussion about the intertwined paths of education and personal growth. We find solace in the vulnerability of these conversations, weaving a bond that transcends the surface of friendship.

Ellie, with her adventurous spirit, inspires discussions about pursuing passions and embracing the unknown. Stargazing sessions become moments of introspection, pondering the vast possibilities that await us beyond the familiar horizon.

Robyn, ever the storyteller, weaves narratives that transport us to fantastical realms. Our imaginations take flight as we envision the extraordinary lives we aspire to lead, each story becoming a stepping stone towards our own narratives.

As the weeks progress, the anticipation for the upcoming lake house trip grows. Shopping for swimsuits becomes a group activity, filled with laughter and friendly debates over fashion choices.

Amidst the excitement, I share stories of my parents' high school love, adding a touch of romance to our discussions. Jameson and I plan activities for our time at the lake, promising each other unforgettable moments.

The nights are filled with bonfires, stargazing, and heart-to-heart talks with friends. Conversations weave a tapestry of shared experiences, creating memories that will linger long after the summer ends.

One weekend, we organize a beach day, building sandcastles, playing beach volleyball, and enjoying the warmth of the sun on our skin. Laughter mingles with the sound of crashing waves as we create snapshots of joy.

Another day, we embark on a hiking expedition, discovering hidden waterfalls and capturing breathtaking views. The scent of pine and the rustling of leaves become the soundtrack to our summer adventures.

At the local fair, we indulge in cotton candy, ride the Ferris wheel, and challenge each other to games of skill. The carousel spins, and laughter fills the air as we revel in the simple joys of summer.

Evenings are spent cooking together, experimenting with recipes, and creating our own culinary masterpieces. The aroma of shared meals becomes a backdrop to the camaraderie and bonds strengthening with each passing day.

As the weeks draw to a close, our conversations shift to reflections on the moments we've shared. We gather around a bonfire one last time, sharing stories, hopes, and a sense of gratitude for the bonds formed.

The anticipation for the lake house trip has evolved into cherished memories, etched into the fabric of our friendship. The thought of the impending departure brings a mix of emotions, but the shared laughter and A week of preparation for the lake house trip unfolds with a buzz of excitement. Additional shopping, packing, and the anticipation of a three-week vacation occupy my days.

Despite recent wardrobe updates, my mom insists on more shopping, expressing her concern for my safety. An intimate conversation reveals her fears, rooted in her own past. Dinner and a movie follow, concluding with a puzzle of fitting new purchases into my suitcase.

Late-night conversations with Jameson become a ritual, as we discuss the lake house itinerary and our shared dreams for the upcoming adventure. The anticipation builds, creating an atmosphere of shared enthusiasm and anticipation.

As midsummer approaches, our days are filled with shared dreams and spontaneous adventures. A day trip to a nearby amusement park unleashes our inner children as we ride roller coasters, indulge in sugary treats, and capture moments of sheer joy.

Nights are dedicated to stargazing, as we lay beneath the expansive sky, sharing stories and contemplating the vastness of the universe. The bond among us deepens, strengthened by the shared wonders of the cosmos.

Conversations meander through topics of life beyond high school, plans for college, and the uncertainties that lie ahead. Each shared dream becomes a bridge connecting us, intertwining our destinies in the fabric of friendship.

Chapter Two

July

Today is the Fourth of July, marking our one-week stay at the lake house tomorrow. The sun, water, and the serene surroundings create a sense of disorientation, accompanied by sporadic chest pressure over the past two days. Perhaps it's just a minor cold coming on.

I finish breakfast, hastily shower, and dress for the day's festivities. Mrs. Rockwell, our host, informs us about the community-wide celebration, including a street fair, concert, fireworks, and more. I slip into a red and blue two-piece under my white lace summer dress, slipping on Birkenstock sandals before joining everyone in the sitting room. Seated next to Becca on the couch, I ask about her current read.

"It's this brutally sad story about friends drifting apart, but secretly, he has loved her. It ends worse than expected," Becca explains, peeking up from the pages as Jameson walks in.

"Good morning, feeling any better?" Jameson inquires, planting a gentle kiss on my forehead.

Shrugging, I reply, "Eh, a little, I guess. Mom wants to take me to the clinic when we get back if I still feel weird." Hoping it's nothing serious, I express my dislike for doctors. Jameson, about to say something, is interrupted by his parents entering, dressed patriotically.

"Good, you're all up and ready! We leave in ten minutes to head into town," Mrs. Rockwell exclaims enthusiastically. Reminding us about sunscreen due to the high UV index, she hurries away.

Becca and I head to the bedroom to pack a small bag, discussing the sad ending of her book. She starts tearing up, exclaiming, "Ugh, I knew it. The author killed him off."

"Hurry up, Becca, mom and dad are already in the car," Jameson calls from the doorway. As she rushes to fix her mascara, I sit on the bed, contemplating the emotional nature of her book choices.

In the car, the holiday traffic extends our ten-minute trip to nearly half an hour. The main street, adorned with red, white, and blue streamers and stars, is bustling with food trucks and carnival games. We meet Mr. Rockwell at a pizza truck, order food, and head to a picnic bench.

Amidst bites of pizza, Becca updates her parents about her college plans, revealing she chose political science as her major for the upcoming second year. After a while, Jameson takes me for a slow dance to the band's cover of Morgan Wallen's "Chasing You." The atmosphere around us becomes a dance of various couples.

"It's crazy," I suddenly remarked to Jameson, catching him off guard. "This time next year, we'll be stressing about getting everything ready for college. What if we don't go to the same college? What if you get accepted to Stanford, and I don't?"

Jameson's phone interrupts him as he begins to respond. "Hello? Yes, Mom. On our way. See you. Love you too." He puts his phone away, saying, "They set up a blanket at the riverfront for the fireworks."

Another interrupted conversation, left hanging in the air. This pattern, mainly around the topic of college, begins to bother me. As the fireworks display starts, I find myself unusually uninterested, my mood dampened by the walk and lingering thoughts.

It's not just the college conversation; there's a growing sense of distance in Jameson's behavior. The unspoken questions and concerns are left unresolved. The first set of fireworks dazzles the night sky, but just as the finale begins, lightheadedness takes over, and everything turns black.

***

The snow blankets the world, creating a winter wonderland. With a day off school, I invite friends over to play in the snow and indulge in hot cocoa. My parents enjoy the fireplace while Mattie and I watch "The Polar Express," my favorite movie.

"Do you think Santa is real?" Mattie asks, sparking a conversation. "Molly Aspen said her parents told her he's made up. I asked my dad, but he ignored it."

Shrugging, I respond, "Sometimes it's better to believe than not."

As we continue watching, Mr. Sinclair and Aunt May arrive with pizza. We feast until our bellies are full, eventually succumbing to sleep.

***

Those were the good old days.

A week and a half ago, I experienced my first seizure. Dad cut his trip short, and Mom rushed to the hospital when Mrs. Rockwell called from the emergency room. Despite inconclusive test results, the doctors attributed it to likely dehydration, prompting my early return home.

Jameson hasn't responded to my messages since their return, and Becca's explanation about his phone falling into the lake feels inadequate. The silence and distance in our relationship intensify, leaving me with a sinking feeling that perhaps coming to the lake house was a mistake.

A knock on my door interrupts my thoughts. Mom and Dad enter slowly, announcing a call from Dr. Karas, requesting us to visit her office for the results. The car ride to the hospital is swift, but the impending news casts a shadow over us. Dr. Karas' office, adorned with big windows and a balcony, seems to amplify the gravity of the situation.

When the doctor finally speaks, her words shatter the plans I had for senior year and the future. "You have lung cancer, Addley."

Dr. Karas' words hang heavy in the air, casting a pall over the room. My parents, their expressions a blend of disbelief and concern, grasp for any semblance of reassurance. The doctor delves into the intricacies of the diagnosis, medical jargon forming an impenetrable barrier around the stark reality.

"Mom, Dad, I... I don't understand," I stammer, my voice barely above a whisper. My mind races, attempting to reconcile the vibrant dreams of senior year with the ominous cloud of lung cancer that now looms.

The car ride back is shrouded in an uneasy silence. The weight of the diagnosis settles in, each passing mile punctuated by the rhythmic hum of tires on the pavement. My parents exchange glances, their attempts at comforting words lost in the heavy silence that envelops us.

In the confines of our home, the walls seem to close in, echoing the unspoken fears. My room, once a sanctuary of dreams and aspirations, now feels like a cage of uncertainties. A hesitant knock precedes my parents' entrance, their faces etched with concern.

Days merge into a blur of medical consultations and attempts to grasp the gravity of the situation. Conversations revolve around treatment options, side effects, and the delicate dance of navigating life with an unwelcome companion named cancer. The strain on family bonds becomes palpable, tested by the uncharted territories of an unexpected journey.

Attempts to communicate with Jameson remain unanswered. Texts linger in the digital void, a testament to the growing distance between us. I find solace in the rhythmic sound of fingers tapping on my phone, though the comfort of his replies remains elusive.

One evening, the sun dips below the horizon, casting a warm glow across my room. In a moment of vulnerability, I reach out again, fingers hesitating over the keys. "Jameson, I need you," I type, each word carrying the weight of unspoken fears and the desire for a familiar presence in the storm.

As the weeks unfold, a juxtaposition emerges between the external world, oblivious to my internal turmoil, and the private battles waged within. Friends, unaware of the invisible thread connecting me to a realm of uncertainty, continue their summer adventures, laughter echoing against the backdrop of a reality forever altered.

Late nights bring a symphony of thoughts, each one a note in the cacophony of uncertainty. The quiet moments become echoes of introspection, punctuated by the irregular rhythm of my own breaths. Against the backdrop of summer's end, I grapple with a reality reshaped by the unwelcome intruder.

Chapter Three

August

Today marked the kickoff of senior year with a mix of excitement and nervous energy, mainly due to cheer captain tryouts. The morning of August 18 had me diving into my usual routine, starting with a soothing shower where my cherry blossom shower gel worked its magic, and my naturally wavy hair got a quick style with a clear elastic and a pearl claw clip.

Choosing an outfit – a cute white denim skirt, a black halter sports top, and white Converse – set the tone for the day. Downstairs, the family and the Sinclairs gathered around the kitchen table, where my mom couldn't help but wear that familiar worried expression she's had since my last doctor's appointment.

I reassured her about my health and the looming cheer captain tryouts, playing the role of the calm one, despite my own worries. Dad, on a sudden "vacation," joined mom in helicopter parenting mode. Mattie, my brother, questioned why anyone would consider homeschooling for me, and I smoothly brushed it off.

Aunt May's concerned words lingered as Mattie and I made a quick escape. We chatted about mundane things, like our new homeroom teacher, Mrs. Berry, and our shared honors English class. I desperately wanted to keep things normal with Mattie, my best friend.

The truth, however, hid beneath the surface of my cheerful facade. For weeks, I pretended to be okay, hiding my struggles and fears. Every day started with tears in the shower and ended with me putting on a brave face for my parents. Mom cried at night, and I yearned to comfort her, but the reality of stage three bronchial adenoma, or lung cancer, hung over our lives.

A conversation with Dr. Han confirmed the diagnosis, and my attempt to navigate the brutal reality of lung cancer brought forth an overwhelming mix of emotions. The odds were grim, and my choices seemed limited, a harsh reality that both my family and I had to face.

In the midst of personal turmoil, high school life continued with the ordinary and the extraordinary. Navigating friendships became a challenge, with Jameson's absence echoing the shifts in our dynamic. The familiar rhythms of school assemblies and mundane conversations provided a comforting backdrop, masking the internal struggles.

The facade crumbled in Mrs. Rockwell's office, where an innocuous conversation unraveled into a tense confrontation. My insistence on maintaining a sense of normalcy clashed with the principal's concern for my well-being, resulting in a heated exchange. This unforeseen clash became a catalyst for my impromptu departure from school premises.

My jeep became a vessel for self-reflection as I grappled with the dissonance between normalcy and impending tragedy. Seeking solace at the Sinclairs' house, I found refuge in Mattie's room and the familiarity of mundane activities.

I stirred from my slumber to find Aunt May standing in the doorway, her gaze fixed on me. "Someone once told me it isn't nice to stare at people," I chuckled, attempting to break the heaviness that hung in the air. She managed a smile and approached me, nudging me to make room before joining me under the cozy blankets.

"I remember when your mom had you. Mainly because I was in the room beside her. I can still hear her yelling in hysterics," Aunt May reminisced, wrapping her arms around me. Her warmth provided a fleeting moment of solace in the otherwise turbulent storm of emotions. "You haven't told him, have you?"

She didn't need to articulate it; she knew. "He is my best friend. I can't lose him," I whispered, my voice trailing off. "I just can't."

"But you are," Aunt May responded, holding me even tighter. A few tears, whether hers or mine, fell onto the blankets. "And he is losing you too. I can't sit here and pretend like I know what you are going through. I can't pretend to feel your pain. I can, however, feel the pain of losing someone I care about."

With those words, I crumbled. "This isn't fair. I exercise and eat healthily, and I have never smoked. I have only ever followed the rules," I managed to say through a fit of coughing. "I'm the one who gets the most brutal cancer there is, and there's nothing anyone can do about it."

In the midst of my emotional unraveling, Mattie's voice echoed through the house. "Mom, are you home?" he shouted, rushing downstairs before I could compose myself. Aunt May and I faced his inquisitive gaze.

"What's going on here?" Mattie asked, concern etched on his face.

"What's going on is you skipping school," May eyed him sternly.

He shrugged, nonchalantly hopping onto the bed with us. "I saw your parents at the school."

I decided to share a fragment of the truth, acknowledging life's difficulties without delving into the specifics.

I yearned to confide in someone, but the fear of being treated like fragile glass held me back.

Aunt May excused herself to prepare lunch, leaving Mattie and me in the quiet embrace of the room. Seeking a brief escape from reality, I put on my all-time favorite movie, "She's The Man." Glancing over at Mattie, I observed his infectious laughter and silent recitation of every line. His green eyes sparkled with mirth, and the unruly black strands of hair begged for a trim. Despite the turmoil, he managed to bring a sense of normalcy.

"I'm going to miss this," I blurted out, my words escaping before my brain could filter them.

He brushed it off casually. "Who knows, maybe we will go to the same college."

"Yeah, maybe."

The weight of the unspoken hung in the air, the impending goodbye casting a shadow over the simplicity of that moment. Mattie's optimism contrasted sharply with the harsh reality that loomed ahead. As the movie played on, we shared laughter and silence, clinging to the familiarity of each other's presence in the face of an uncertain future.

***

Friday morning unfolded with the unwelcome intrusion of my parents into my cocoon of sleep, ushering in another day of hospital visits and the familiar routine of lab work. Despite the relentless drumbeat of reality, my parents, particularly my mom, clung to a fragile hope that danced just out of reach. In contrast, my dad, a seasoned navigator of medical challenges, stood silently by, bearing witness to the impending tempest.

The belated revelation of my condition, caught in its advanced stages, left me with a mere eighteen percent chance of a semblance of normalcy. Desperate to defy the grim prognosis, we embarked on a whirlwind tour of countless doctors, seeking second, third, and fourth opinions. My dad, a diligent professional in his own right, even scrutinized my scans, hoping to uncover a glimmer of optimism.

Amidst this medical odyssey, my mom clung to denial as a protective shield, warding off the harsh truth she so fervently wished to avoid – the specter of losing another child. The fruitless pursuit of a solution, whether through chemotherapy or a barrage of tests, echoed through our lives, reverberating in hollow corridors.

"I don't understand why I have to keep being poked and prodded. No amount of testing will change the outcome," I muttered, my words perhaps lost to the silence of the room or absorbed by the walls, which bore witness to my mounting frustration.

My pleas to avoid the hospital became a futile refrain in the orchestration of our new normal – a routine where my desires and needs were eclipsed by my parents' insistence, forging a surreal dance of reluctant compliance.

Within the sterile walls of Dr. Han's office, the air hung heavy with anticipation. My dad, the voice of reason, attempted to impose a semblance of normalcy on a situation that had long deviated from the expected course.

Dr. Han's entrance marked the commencement of another round of discussions, a delicate ballet around the deteriorating state of my health. The formalities exchanged between him and my parents painted a veneer of civility over the palpable tension in the room.

"Good morning, Mr. and Mrs. McRae," Dr. Han greeted, extending a hand in a gesture that belied the weight of the impending conversation. "Hello, Addley. How are you feeling?"

A bitter laugh escaped my lips. "Well, I am dying, and my parents won't accept it, so they drag me here every other day to be tested on like an animal. Feeling great, let me tell you," I quipped, my eyes rolling in a theatrical display of sarcasm.

Sensing the frustration in the room, Dr. Han tactfully suggested my parents step outside. My mom, in a half-hearted attempt to protest, yielded to the relief apparent on my face.

"I'm not angry; I am annoyed. They won't listen," I expressed, the simmering emotions threatening to breach the surface. The impending discussion about treatment plans loomed, intensifying my frustration.

As Dr. Han broached the delicate subject, I met his gaze with a mixture of resignation and defiance. "There is no treatment plan. My chances are so low it's not even funny," I declared, my gaze drifting towards the door. "They mean the world to me. But I can't subject myself to more than a body should bear, knowing it's failing me anyway."

A pamphlet, a cruel twist of fate, materialized in Dr. Han's hands with the title "Chemotherapy Saves Lives." The absurdity of the statement triggered genuine laughter, a poignant acknowledgment of life's bitter irony.

"We will go about this in the way you want to, but I think you should at least try—" Dr. Han began, only to be interrupted by my resolute cut-off.

"I know how it works. I know the outcome. Not trying is better than failing," I asserted, standing up and handing back the pamphlet. "Thank you. Please try to get my parents on board. The sooner, the better."

With those words, I walked out, leaving behind the sterile echoes of the office. The corridor stretched ahead, symbolizing the uncertain path that awaited, a journey where choices were limited, and acceptance became the only steadfast companion.

The corridor stretched out before me, a metaphorical path winding through the uncertainties of my future. With each step, the sterile confines of the hospital office retreated, leaving behind the hushed whispers of medical conversations. The weight of my impending reality pressed upon my shoulders, a constant companion on this lonely journey.

Exiting Dr. Han's office felt like stepping from one realm into another. The muted beige of the hospital walls gave way to the brighter hues of the hallway, a deceptive contrast to the darkness that loomed within. The aroma of disinfectant clung to the air, a scent that had become synonymous with my existence.

My parents, their faces etched with concern, awaited my return. Their eyes, searching for answers, reflected the internal struggle mirrored in my own. I had just relinquished my stance on treatment, a decision met with both understanding and resistance.

Dr. Han emerged, his expression a blend of professionalism and empathy. He ushered my parents into his office, a sacred space where discussions about my deteriorating health unfolded like a tragic narrative. I leaned against the wall, allowing the cool surface to provide a momentary respite from the emotional tempest within.

The corridor became a passage of reflection, a space where the echoes of conversations lingered. The muffled voices from adjacent rooms whispered tales of pain and resilience, a reminder that my struggle was not unique. As I waited, the weight of my decisions settled, mingling with the scent of antiseptic.

When my parents finally emerged from the office, their faces carried a mix of somber understanding and lingering hope. Dr. Han, a bridge between the medical realm and our human experience, had imparted a sense of clarity that left no room for false illusions.

The drive back home was laden with silence, each occupant of the car lost in their own thoughts. The passing scenery blurred into a tableau of fleeting moments, the outside world indifferent to the inner turmoil of our hearts.

Upon arriving home, the familiar sights held an undertone of poignancy. The living room, once a haven of family gatherings, now bore witness to a silent acknowledgment of our shared pain. The photos on the wall, frozen smiles capturing moments of joy, served as a bittersweet reminder of what once was.

I retreated to my room, seeking solace in the familiar surroundings. The walls, adorned with remnants of a life untouched by the looming shadow, provided a sanctuary where I could grapple with the reality I had chosen. My thoughts spiraled, dancing between acceptance and defiance.

Mattie's voice, a welcome interruption, echoed through the hallway. He had come, unbidden but instinctively aware of the storm raging within. His presence brought a fleeting sense of normalcy, a reprieve from the weighty decisions that loomed over me.

"Hey," he greeted, his eyes searching mine for a trace of vulnerability. The unspoken understanding between us enveloped the room, transcending the need for words. We shared a moment, a silent communion that acknowledged the fragility of life and the strength found in shared burdens.

As the day unfolded, the sun dipped below the horizon, casting a warm glow that painted the sky in hues of pink and gold. The world outside continued its relentless march, indifferent to the struggles within our walls.

Evening descended, enveloping the house in a gentle quiet. The air, heavy with unspoken truths, hung between my parents and me. The kitchen, once alive with the aroma of shared meals, now stood as a witness to the silence that pervaded our interactions.

I retreated to the solace of my room, the sanctuary where I could grapple with the weight of my decisions. The night unfolded, a tapestry woven with the threads of contemplation and acceptance. The soft glow of a bedside lamp cast shadows on the walls, each flicker a testament to the undulating emotions that ebbed and flowed within.

In the stillness of the night, a profound realization settled upon me — the journey ahead would be defined not only by the choices made but also by the resilience to face the inevitable with grace. As sleep beckoned, I embraced the uncertainty, a silent vow to navigate the uncharted path with courage and, perhaps, a glimmer of hope.

Chapter Four

September

The first day of the month rolled in, a sweet Saturday urging me to sit down and weave a tapestry of dreams in the form of a bucket list. Mom and dad, in their own way, had nodded in acceptance of the decisions I've made. Well, as much as they could, given the circumstances.

Amidst the quiet contemplation of my aspirations, a buzzing symphony erupted from my phone. A constant reminder that it had been a week since I ended things with Jameson. He's still desperately trying to deny the undeniable, throwing words against the evidence I've seen with my own eyes— pictures and videos that laid bare his betrayal.

But you know what? I've reached a point where I just don't care anymore. It feels like both of us had checked out of that relationship a while back. You can't force someone to stay, to want you. I've come to terms with that bitter truth. So, with a deliberate move, I silenced my phone, reclaiming the tranquility needed to dive back into my bucket list.

The ink flowed as I penned down dreams of sunrise adventures, spontaneous road trips, heartwarming gatherings with friends, and the simple joy of getting lost in the pages of a beloved book. Each entry became a piece of my heart, a commitment to a life unburdened by the ghosts of the past.

As I let my pen dance across the pages, something magical happened—the weight of recent decisions started to lift. The bucket list transformed into more than just wishes on paper; it became a promise to live, to savor every moment within the limitations of time and circumstance.

With the final dream jotted down, I closed the notebook. The room's quietude wrapped around me, and in that stillness, I sensed the first whispers of a journey that transcends the ticking clock and the twists of fate.

Try Alcohol

Homecoming Queen

Plant a rose garden

"Oh, what's this?" Mattie appears out of thin air and snatches my notepad before I can protest. "Addley's Bucket List." He reads it out loud with that teasing smirk of his. "Little early to make one of these, don't you think, Addie?"

I snatch the notepad back and stuff it into my desk, shooting him a defiant look. "It's never too early to dream big and slay those goals," I retort, throwing in some extra flair because, well, why not?

My condition might be hurrying things along, but that doesn't mean I'm backing down. Not that I'd be able to tick everything off anyway. Thanks to my newfound popularity with doctors, I'm on a first-name basis with the waiting room. Regular checkups have become as routine as morning coffee.

Just a few days ago, Dr. Karas dropped the bomb that the cancer is on a sprint through my body. Dr. Han, ever the bearer of blunt news, hinted at a one-year deadline. Reality check, much?

Meanwhile, Mattie sprawls on my bed, hanging out with Sprinkles the fish like it's just another day. I take a mental trip down memory lane, remembering the day I got that aquatic diva. Oh, high school – where bucket lists collide with doctor appointments, and Sprinkles becomes the unofficial mascot of my teenage drama.

*****

"Addie, seriously! The moms are throwing serious shade our way, and the swings are calling our names. Can't resist the swing magic, right?" *Mattie's puppy-dog eyes plead with me as he attempts another gentle tug. "And, for the record, those rigged games are practically the carnival's way of testing our determination."*

I flash a playful grin and counter, "I'm not one to back down from a glittery challenge, especially when it involves a fish of this caliber!" My finger dramatically points to the twinkling wonder hanging above the game, the epitome of glitter-infused cuteness.

Mattie, feigning a look of horror, digs into his pocket and pulls out a victorious five-dollar bill. "You and your sparkly whims have officially won," he declares, surrendering to the allure of the carnival game and secretly enjoying the whole glittery escapade.

So there we are, in the midst of carnival chaos, chasing sunsets, and adding a splash of sparkle to our teenage adventures. Because, really, what's life without a bit of glitter and a cute fish to prove that sometimes, the most delightful victories come in the most unexpected, sparkly packages?

***

"Ugh, four years ago feels like ancient history," I sigh, gazing at the glittery fish in my hands. "You won this for me, and all you could talk about for days was how you missed out on the swings that day."

Mattie grins, plopping the fish on the bed before joining me. "What's the scoop, Addie? Spill the tea. It's been weeks, and I'm ready to be your drama llama. Jameson drama, right? Forget that dude. He wasn't worth your time. In fact, no one is!" He looks down, muttering almost to himself, "Especially not him." I barely catch his mumbled comment.

I want to lay it all out there.

I need to let him in on my secret.

But when I try to speak, my words get tangled in my throat, and at that exact moment, Mr. Sinclair announces the food's ready. "We'll chat about it later."

***

With the grilling done, we huddle around the fire pit, marshmallows in hand, creating s'mores magic. Dad and Mattie dive into soccer and college discussions, and for the first time in months, my parents wear genuine smiles. It's a scene I've sorely missed. Dad's pranks were legendary, like the time he scared the bejeezus out of Kenny with a Grudge-inspired stunt. Even now, Grudge movie posters give me the creeps.

As midnight approaches, the Sinclairs head home, but Mattie suggests a twist to our usual sleepover— it's treehouse time. "I can't believe this thing is still standing," he marvels. The treehouse has weathered storms and a few mini-tornadoes.

We spend the night swapping stories about our younger selves, reminiscing about the days when the most significant decision was choosing between chocolate or strawberry ice cream. The next morning, I wake up to the sound of Mattie's adorable snores. His hair is a tousled mess, lips forming a half-frown. I can't help but wonder about his dreams.

"I sense your stare," he whispers, eyes still closed. I respond with a fake snore, yanking the blanket over my head. Of course, he laughs, prompting a laugh from me too.

I'm going to miss these moments.

Do people only realize how much they miss something when it's gone?

Amidst the laughter, a peculiar warmth fills the air. My chest flutters, and just before everything goes dark, the last vivid images in my mind are of us covered in blood—yet, in that moment, all I can think about is the laughter that came before.

***

So, Kenny and Paxton kind of insisted on one last beach house bash before it closes for the year. And, uh, I'm starting at Peakview High next week with my siblings. The nerves are real.

Been thinking of trying out cheer this year. Kenny did it her freshman year before ditching, claiming she met her bestie through it or whatever.

Paxton, being the designated driver, made a pit stop at the gas station. "Refreshments," he says, all casual.

He comes back with these brown bags, and I should've seen it coming. All summer, they've been plotting the first senior kickoff party. Mom and dad vetoed it, obviously.

Kenny checks the bags, giggling, "Good starter, but we're hitting the liquor store later."

Feeling awkward, they give me this look. Paxton breaks the silence, handing me a diet Pepsi. I mean, thanks, I guess.

It's pushing eleven, and I'm sprawled on my bed pretending to read. The party is going wild, and I'm surprised the cops haven't crashed it yet. The twins invited me to join, but seriously, alcohol at our age? No thanks. Plus, hanging out with a bunch of senior-class goofballs isn't my vibe.

I barely finish the book as the party slowly winds down. Only the twins, Paxton's girlfriend, and Kenny's bestie stick around.

Switching off my light, I drift into sleep, but it's a struggle. Can't stay asleep for more than twenty minutes at a stretch.

The next morning, my room is invaded by cops and my parents. Kenny drowned in the ocean while I was knocked out, and Paxton? Who even knows where he is.

***

My eyes flutter open, and there's this strange taste in my mouth. Dad and Mattie are huddled together in the corner, expressions heavy. Mom and Aunt May look concerned in the hallway. I try to speak, but something's blocking my words.

Dad signals for the doctor, who removes the tubing, offering a sip of water. "Can you tell me your name and birthday?" the doctor inquires.

Shaking my head, I rasp out, "Addley Rose Mcrae," and take another sip. "My birthday is September sixteenth. What happened?"

"Your cancer is spreading, Addley," the doctor discloses, casting a pall over the room. "You're lucky your friend was there; you almost suffocated on your blood."

I turn to Mattie, still wearing his bloodied pajamas. Everyone else leaves the room, leaving just him. Pulling up a chair, he sits next to me.

"I shouldn't have asked you to sleep in the tree house," he mutters, his voice filled with regret.

Trying to comfort him, I say, "It's not your fault. You didn't know." My fingers fidget nervously as he continues.

Taking a deep breath, Mattie confesses, "I did know. A few days before school started, I overheard our moms talking late. Mom was trying to calm your mom down. I was waiting for you to tell me."

"I wanted to," I admit.

He rises, enveloping me in a hug. "I know." The room feels heavy with unspoken words, and a bittersweet sadness hangs in the air.

***

After six days, they finally let me escape the hospital's clutches.

A week of bed rest awaits me at home, with a half-hearted suggestion for homeschooling. But let's be real, that's not my style.

Mom's whipping up her famous tomato soup, a throwback to my childhood sick days. The nostalgia stings a bit, especially now when there's no magical recovery in sight.

The familiar buzz of my phone interrupts my thoughts, and, on autopilot, I answer before glancing at the caller ID.

"Hey, Addie, heard you're not feeling great. Anything I can bring over? Still into sprite and rolls when you're under the weather?" It's Jameson.

I give an involuntary head shake, forgetting he can't see me. "Just stop, okay? No more calls, no more texts. We're done," I assert before hanging up.

Enough with the drama; none of this will matter in the grand scheme anyway.

Later, like clockwork, Mattie swings by after soccer, just like he's been doing every day since I got home. We retreated to my room, streaming Peakview's football game.

I decided to part ways with cheer for now. It hurts, but I want to fill my remaining days with the dreams I've always held close.

I doze off during halftime, and when I wake up the next morning, I find myself tucked under the blankets with a note from Mattie.

> *Had to head home so call*

> *me when you wake up!*

> *-Mattie*

I glance at the clock, and it's just a tad past eight in the morning, so I figure I'll bask in the morning vibes a bit longer. A luxurious bubble bath calls my name, and I soak in its warmth for nearly an hour, enjoying every blissful minute.

As I step into my room, a poorly wrapped gift box catches my eye, perched on my bed alongside another one of Mattie's adorable notes.

> *Put this on and meet me out*

> *Dont ask questions*

> *-Mattie*

Aye aye, captain.

With eager anticipation, I tear into the box, revealing a pair of sleek black leggings and a vintage-looking cream-colored t-shirt. It's the very one I've been eyeing in Mattie's closet for ages, and he's finally caved. Swiftly, I change into the outfit, throw on my white Converse, and descend the stairs, ready to share my plans with my parents.

Predictably, they attempt to thwart my adventurous spirit with reminders of doctor's orders. "You should be in bed," they insist.

"I've been cooped up for almost two weeks. Two weeks too long, might I add," I retort, locking eyes with them. "I don't want to spend whatever time I have left strapped to my bed or the couch. Love you guys." After a round of hugs, I snatch my keys and jacket, prepared for my mini escapade.

And there's Mattie, leaning casually against my jeep, donned in fitted black sweatpants and a grey hoodie featuring a picture of us from our younger years – a Christmas gift from two years ago.

"Hop in, I'm driving," he declares, snatching my keys and ushering me to the passenger seat. The note explicitly instructed me not to ask questions, but my curiosity prevails.

"Can we get food? I'm starving," I inquire, and as if on cue, my belly emits a loud growl, sparking a shared fit of laughter between us.

***

Today is just one of those perfect days.

I close my eyes, savoring the gentle breeze wafting through the open windows, signaling the enchanting shift from summer to fall. The leaves outside have adopted a mesmerizing burnt orange hue. The air carries a crispness that calls for a light jacket, yet it's warm enough to forgo one.

As I soak in the delightful weather, my thoughts meander to what everyone might be doing this time next year. Will Dad continue his travels, or perhaps even increase them? Is Paxton going to be the pillar of support Mom and Dad need? I really hope so.

Then, my mind wanders to Mattie. What college will he choose? Has he found new friends or even stumbled upon the love of his life? A solitary tear escapes as I contemplate the prospect of him slowly forgetting me.

Mattie's voice breaks through my reverie, bringing me back to the present. "Two hash browns, an egg muffin, and coffee, right?" I hadn't even realized we'd parked. I nod in agreement, resting my head against the car door.

The idea of not being around anymore is hard to fathom. We spend our lives envisioning the future, knowing our aspirations, who we want to be, and where we hope to end up.

Mattie hands me our breakfast delights, and we settle into a conversation that spans everything and nothing for what feels like an eternity. He tidies up the empty wrappers, buckles up, and announces, "Long drive, get comfortable," unveiling a snug blanket from the back seat.

I think about asking where we're headed but decide against it. If Mattie wants to whisk me away on a secret adventure, I'm all in, eager to play by his rules.

Three hours into our road trip, Mattie makes a pit stop at a gas station for refueling and snacks. Seeing an opportunity, I unlock my phone to find a cascade of notifications.

32 missed calls, 59 texts.

The missed calls are mostly Mom and Dad, with Ellie throwing in one attempt, and Jameson persistently ringing three times. Deciding to quell the concern, I tap the call button next to Mom's name.

She answers with palpable worry in her voice, "Oh god, you better be okay, Addley," practically shouting through the phone.

I nod instinctively, forgetting she can't see me. "I'm sorry, Mom. I turned my phone off and fell asleep," I offer reassurance.

"Addley, you can't be doing stuff like this right now, not with what's happening. Your dad and I are worried sick over here. Where are you?"

Just as I'm about to answer, Mattie returns to the car, shooting me a curious 'what's up' expression. I silently mouth 'Mom' to him, prompting him to take my phone and step outside.

Mattie engages in what feels like an eternity of conversation with Mom. When he finally rejoins me in the car, he hands back my phone with the most radiant smile. "It's been settled," he declares before buckling up and steering us back into the drive.

Where to? Well, that's still a mystery, and I'm loving every second of this teenage adventure with Mattie by my side.

***

"Kids, stop bickering and hop into bed. We've got an early start tomorrow," Aunt May scolded Mattie and me as we playfully argued about who gets the left side of the bed.

Tomorrow, we're going on an airplane for the first time! I'm a little scared, but Mom said everything will be fine, and I trust her. Why? Because it's our seventh birthday celebration, and we're going to Disney World! We'll stay in Cinderella's castle for the whole week. I can't wait to tell all my friends— they'll be so jealous!

Beside me, Mattie lets out a little groan. "Your birthday's sooner. You can have this spot."

Aunt May smiles as she tucks us in and turns off the lights. "Thank you, Addie," Mattie whispers, his voice barely audible.

I nod and flip onto my belly. "Hey, Addie."

I muffle a sleepy 'yeah?' as he continues, "Promise me we'll always be best friends?"

That night, under the soft glow of the nightlight, we sealed our friendship with a pinkie promise— promising each other a lifetime of being best friends.

***

"Wake up, princess. We're finally here," I feel Mattie gently shaking me from my slumber.

Yawning and stretching, I reluctantly open my eyes, squinting to check the time on my phone. It's nearly six in the morning, and I realize Mattie has been behind the wheel for well over twelve hours.

"Where are we?" I inquire, my voice groggy from sleep.

With a mischievous grin, Mattie guides me to our hotel room, emphasizing that it's a surprise. He heads back to the car to retrieve the bags, a thoughtful gesture I hadn't even noticed in my half-asleep state.

As Mattie hauls in the last suitcase, he lets out a massive yawn. "I'm setting an alarm. Don't even think about touching it in the morning. Top secret," he warns, giving me a playful side-eye.

After preparing for a well-deserved rest, Mattie turns off the lights. "Goodnight, Mattie," I murmur as I settle into bed, still curious about the surprise awaiting us in the morning.

***

Mattie's alarm jingles at the delightful hour of twelve in the afternoon, shattering the peaceful cocoon of our hotel room. While he's been drifting in the blissful embrace of dreams, I've been awake since eight-thirty, navigating the quiet realms of my phone.

Ignoring the strict mandate not to disturb the alarm, I decide to intervene, joyously springing from my bed to Mattie's. He groans, playfully swatting at me.

"You weigh a ton," he quips, laughter infusing his words. In response, I mischievously shove a pillow in his direction. Weight loss, wheeziness, chest pains —unwanted companions on my cancer journey. Yet, amidst the heaviness, Mattie's playful spirit provides a comforting balm.

Finally victorious over the alarm, I seize the chance to plead, "Please, Mattie, tell me where we are." On my knees, eyes pleading, I look up at him. Gently pushing me away, Mattie nods toward the bathroom.

Approaching cautiously, I open the door to discover a scene that brings tears to my eyes. "Happy Birthday, Addie," Mattie declares, his face lit up with pure joy. The bathroom has transformed into a magical haven adorned with balloons and flowers—a celebration I was too engrossed in my illness to realize.

"I missed your birthday. I am so sorry, I'm so selfish," Mattie confesses, remorse coloring his words. The tears, held back for too long, now stream freely.

The realization dawns on me—Friday night, his visit wasn't just about the game. It was his birthday, our tradition being to spend our birthdays together.

Mattie wraps me in a comforting hug. "You have a very valid reason. I don't care about my birthday; I care about spending time with my best friend." Gently pushing me away, he maintains a reassuring grip on my shoulders. "Now, go get ready. Disney awaits."

On the bathroom counter, a thoughtful ensemble awaits—leggings, Nikes, a Minnie Mouse birthday shirt, and matching birthday ears. Dressed and ready after brushing my teeth, I find Mattie donning a coordinating birthday shirt and ears.

"We only have today; tomorrow we head back. Your mom wouldn't let you miss any more school," he notes, and with that, we embark on our enchanting adventure to the park, leaving behind a room filled with the echoes of laughter and tears of overwhelming joy.

***

As the sun dipped below the horizon, casting hues of orange and pink across the sky, Mattie and I reveled in the magical realms of Disney for hours on end. Amid laughter, sugary treats, and the thrill of whimsical rides, our hearts soared. Yet, as the clock ticked on, the day's adventures left a gentle weariness in my chest, whispering sweet lullabies of rest.

When Mattie, his eyes reflecting sincerity and friendship, admitted that all he desired was to cherish these moments with his best friend, a realization dawned on me. In this fleeting passage of time, more than ever, it became imperative to be the friend he deserved, ensuring every shared second was etched into the fabric of our memories.

"Let's find a cozy spot to take a break," he suggested, sensing the quiet fatigue settling in. "We have somewhere to be in twenty minutes. I promise we can leave after." His pinky finger extended towards me, a silent pact sealed in a familiar exchange.

***

Blindfolded and guided by trust, I followed Mattie, each step heightening the anticipation of our next adventure. "Have we arrived yet?" my impatience surfaced, a playful protest against the mysterious unknown.

"Shush, child. Stop being so impatient," he teased.

As the journey came to a pause, Mattie removed the blindfold, urging me to keep my eyes closed until the awaited cue.

"Open," he whispered sweetly into my ear.

Tutto Italia Ristorante.

Italy.

Disney World.

"You stole my bucket list," I exclaimed with eyes brimming with watery delight. This emotional overflow hadn't visited me since the days of infancy or the heartache of Kenny's passing.

Mattie, with an unabashed nod, confessed, "Of course I did, and I'll make sure we check off every item before time slips away." He wrapped me in a warm hug.

In that heartwarming moment, a cascade of reflections overwhelmed me. Was I unknowingly taking Mattie's extraordinary friendship for granted? Has he always been this incredibly remarkable? Without a shadow of a doubt, he was the best friend I could have ever dreamed of.

We relished the most exquisite meal, weaving memories into each delightful bite. As we returned to the hotel, with the clock ticking just before eleven, my eyes gently fell shut, surrendering to the embrace of a profound and blissful sleep—a respite, the sweetest I had experienced in months.

Chapter Five

October

Three months have breezed by since my world took a nosedive after that surprise seizure, unveiling an unexpected plot twist – a life-changing diagnosis. The Sinclairs and my folks are the sole bearers of this secret, a pact of silence I've willingly embraced, at least until my brother Paxton returns for fall break in November. A phone call won't cut it, especially when Paxton's allergic to anything resembling a conversation.

Trudging through the halls during the second period, I'm shackled by the weight of honors English. Sure, I've maintained straight A's in other classes, but this particular subject, recommended by my counselor for college brownie points, feels like a textbook case of irony. What's the point of accumulating college credit when my life's heading south?

Mrs. Berry's voice pulls me back to reality – my turn to present the wonders of bilingual brilliance.

Mid-sentence, a splash of crimson lands on my note cards, a poignant reminder of my newfound fragility. With an apologetic mumble, I sprint to the bathroom, my nose unleashing a full-on crimson waterfall. Toilet paper becomes my makeshift knight against the blood tide as I slide down the wall, embracing the chill of the cold floor.

Enter Ellie, armed with makeup wipes and a whirlwind of concern. "What happened in there?" she exclaims, wiping away the evidence of my bodily rebellion. Fidgeting with my fingers, I confess, "Don't be mad, I'm sick. Like, really really sick. I have cancer." As the weight of my words settles, Ellie's big brown eyes fill with tears that threaten to flood the hallway.

"How? Why?" Her words stumble, mirroring the chaos in her mind. I weave the tale of my recent struggles – the lake incident, the breakup with Jameson, and the silent battles that kept me away from school.

Amid shared tears and whispered words, my nose finally grants me reprieve. Tossing blood-soaked tissues aside, I head to the gym locker for a costume change, assuring Ellie I'll catch up. Turning a corner, I collide with Jameson, who's greeted by the crimson evidence on my shirt. With a whisper about the nosebleed, dizziness sets in, and I'm swallowed by the comforting embrace of darkness.

***

"Addie, you look like a princess in that dress!" Mattie twirled me around, making my dress swish. The eighth-grade Sadie Hawkins dance is coming up, and I worked up the courage to ask Bradley Harris to be my date. His mom was supposed to pick me up, but there's a delay. Mom went to call Bradley's mom to coordinate, and when she returned, her expression foretold impending trouble.

"I'm sorry, Addley. Mrs. Harris wasn't aware you were his date. Something about a different girl." Oh. "That's okay; I didn't care to go much anyway." I put on a brave smile, masking the disappointment. If Bradley didn't want to go with me, that's fine – just don't leave me hanging.

"Well, Aunt May, you should get Mattie to the school. I'm going to change into some sweats. Love you, guys." I started heading up the stairs. "Have fun, Mattie."

***

Beep. Beep. Beep. Beep.

The rhythmic beeping of the hospital machines created a soundtrack to my life that I wished I could skip. My eyes fluttered open, and the stark reality of yet another hospital room greeted me. Jameson, my ever-present friend, was by my side, concern etched on his face.

"You seized again at school," he explained, recounting the chaotic events that led us here. Mom had sprung into action, clearing the hallways, and now the hospital was my unscheduled pitstop. My parents had scurried off to talk with the doctors, leaving Jameson to navigate the hospital drama with me.

My throat felt drier than the Sahara, and Jameson, always attentive, adjusted the pillow behind me and handed me a cup of water – my liquid salvation. I gulped it down, faster than a high school rumor spreading through the halls, offering a mumbled 'thank you,' to which he responded with a friendly nod.

As we sat in a contemplative silence, my parents and Dr. Han made their entrance, the latter exclaiming, "My favorite patient!" The doctor, armed with charts, went on about my recent seizure and an unexpected nosebleed during class.

Interrupting before the medical revelations went too far, I issued a directive, "Leave the room. Everyone." The door closed behind them. "Mom, dad, please, don't say anything. Please?" They nodded understandingly.

Turning to Dr. Han, I cut straight to the chase, "What do I have to do to make it to the homecoming dance on Saturday?"

Dr. Han, perched on the edge of the bed, sported a contemplative frown. He grappled with delivering news he knew I might not like. "Your health is too compromised, Addley. You shouldn't even be going to school."

With a determined gleam in my eyes, I began, "I don't have infinite time on this planet, nobody does, but my time has been reduced majorly. I know I'm going to die, and sooner than I thought. I want to live what life I have left. Not be scared of every turn I make. I'm weak, and my health is declining, I understand that, but I refuse to spend the rest of my so-called life in a hospital bed. When the time comes, and I have to go, I want to die knowing I did stuff I love. Spent time with the people I enjoy. Not smelling like rubbing alcohol."

As the words escaped my lips, I wiped away the unbidden tears. "So, please, when can I leave?"

Dr. Han sighed, realizing that the strength in my plea echoed the fierce desire to make the most of the moments I had left. "Addley, we'll work on a plan. But, you need to promise to take it easy, okay?"

I nodded, the prospect of escaping the sterile hospital walls amplifying the sparkle in my eyes.

Homecoming, with all its teenage magic, awaited, and I was determined to embrace it with open arms.

***

Doctor Han released me the next morning, his exhaustive talks about safety and hospital rules still echoing in my ears. I understood the precautions, but I had made it clear – I wasn't about to spend my days bored out of my mind in a hospital bed.

As part of our agreement, I conceded to skip homecoming, much to my chagrin. A small sacrifice for the larger goal of evading the watchful eyes of the medical staff. Cancer had already claimed my spot in the cheerleading squad, and now it was robbing me of a teenage rite of passage.

Mom and dad, understanding my craving for normalcy, took me to McDonald's on the way home. Despite my dwindling appetite, the thought of a ten-piece chicken nugget and their savory ranch sauce had me yearning for the familiar taste.

Once home, I headed upstairs for a comforting soak in the bath. The water, enriched with bath salts and bubble bath, provided a brief respite from the medical whirlwind. I lost myself in a book, the chapters a welcome escape from the reality that loomed over me.

The tranquility of the bath was interrupted when Jameson unexpectedly invaded my room, turning on the lamp and nearly giving me a heart attack with his surprise appearance. Recovering, I ushered him out, insisting on some privacy to get dressed.

After donning a pair of leggings and a baggy band tee, I welcomed Jameson back into my room. However, I set the boundaries clear – no discussions about the recent hospital episode. We could talk about anything else.

Pulling out my desk chair, Jameson joined me on the bed. He tentatively broached the subject of 'us,' a topic that carried the weight of past betrayals. I acknowledged the reality – there was no 'us' anymore, not after he cheated and we drifted apart.

His apology was met with a surprising calmness on my end. Anger had already been spent, and I understood the inevitability of our separation.

However, Jameson expressed genuine concern about my well-being, unaware of the seizures that had recently become a part of my life.

Scooting over, I patted the bed, inviting him to lay down. I shared a lighthearted laugh about the seizures occurring only in his presence, and we decided to take a break from reality by watching a movie.

Jameson kicked off his shoes, grabbed the remote, and we settled in to watch Harry Potter. The familiar tale of wizardry and friendship provided a welcome escape, and during the second movie, Jameson succumbed to slumber. I covered us with blankets and, feeling the weight of illness, allowed myself a brief nap.

Being sick had taken a toll, not just physically, but emotionally and socially. In these stolen moments of normalcy, I found solace, surrounded by the fictional magic of Hogwarts and the genuine warmth of a friend who, despite the rocky past, was there in that vulnerable moment.

***

Mom jolted us awake around five for dinner, giving us a subtle nod as she exited the room. In the midst of Jameson's apologies for drifting off on me, my phone belted out a familiar ring.

It was Mattie.

Guilt flooded me; I hadn't talked to him since school yesterday. Quick to answer, I blurted, "Hey, I'm sorry. I haven't been ignoring you. I—"

He cut me off with an annoyed tone, "Napping with the enemy. I know."

Raising a finger, I motioned to the door, silently pleading for some privacy. "It's not like that. We fell asleep watching movies," I explained, unsure why I felt the need to justify myself. "You know my predicament. I refuse to leave this earth with bad blood between anyone."

A sigh echoed through the phone. "I just don't want to see my best friend get hurt again. Especially now," Mattie expressed his concern.

I understood his worry, but my situation was different. "I am going to die. My lungs have already betrayed me. I just want to live what life I have left carefree. Understand that?"

We continued our conversation until Mom sent Jameson to fetch me for dinner. The dining table became a battleground for Dad's questions about Jameson's post-graduation plans, the colleges he'd applied to, and the exciting prospects I would never experience.

"Still hoping to see Addley at Stanford with me next year," Jameson nudged me, and I could only nod and smile. Mom excused herself, the weight of unspoken sadness lingering in her eyes as she cleared the table.

She didn't bring it up as often now. My decision not to pursue treatment had broken her, I could tell. I never meant to hurt her, but I faced the reality of the odds, and they weren't in my favor. At all.

Moving to the sink, I grabbed a stool to help Mom with the plates. Whispering to her so Jameson couldn't hear, I reassured, "I'm not doing this to hurt you."

Mom was already fighting back tears when I sat down. "I know. It's hard, sweetie. First Kendall and now you. Really makes a parent wonder where they went wrong." I enveloped Mom in a comforting hug, a poignant reversal of roles from the times when she used to be the one soothing me through my pain.

"You guys are truly the best parents ever. Sometimes God needs others more than people on earth do."

Mom beamed at me. "Your PopPop used to drop wisdom bombs like that when I was your age. You've got quite the smarts, kiddo."

After our little heart-to-heart, Jameson took off, and Dad went on an ice cream run, leaving Mom and me to set up for a cozy movie night.

Back in the day, every Friday after dinner meant slipping into the comfiest PJs. Dad would inflate the air mattress, Mom would whip up the popcorn, and Aunt May would bring out the cookie magic. We'd dive into a movie marathon, staying up way past bedtime.

Fast forward thirty minutes, and there we were, all in our PJs. Mom and Dad claimed the couch, leaving me on the air mattress.

Around 2 a.m., my parents dozed off. I decided to power down the TV and cocoon myself in a cozy blanket.

I'm dog-tired, but there's this fear of losing out on moments. I wish I had someone to talk to, someone who gets what I'm going through.

No one warns you about the lonely abyss when you're facing a terminal situation. Mom and Dad are losing a daughter, and Mattie is losing a friend, but I'm the one losing my life, and it's a heavier burden than I let on.

Some nights I feel like I'm suffocating, from my not-so-great lungs or from the anxiety.

Here's a secret I won't confess to anyone: I'm utterly terrified.

Cancer wasn't part of the grand plan I had for my future. I try to stay strong for everyone, but when left alone with my thoughts, tears find their way out. Not just for my condition, but the collective weight of everyone's tears is dragging me down.

Enough with the pity party. It's time to sleep; tomorrow is homecoming, and with the football team's victory tonight, I bet tomorrow night will be wild.

I won't be there, keeping my promise to Dr. Han, but I want to catch a glimpse of my friends all dressed up with their dates.

The next morning, the aroma of bacon, eggs, and waffles fills the air. The room is tidied from last night's festivities, and instead of the floor, I find myself on the couch.

After a good stretch, I fold my blanket. Sounds of chatter emanate from the dining room; I head that way. But when I try to open the door, it's locked.

Knocking, I call out, "I can hear you."

Silence.

Whoever's inside stops talking.

No worries; I'll just sneak in through the kitchen entrance.

Correction.

The joke's on me again; they managed to lock this door too.

However, this time there's a note on the door.

> *Momma Mal made breakfast, meet*
>
> *me in the treehouse*
>
> *-Mattie*

I step outside, the note cradled in my hands as I embark on the petite climb up the ladder to the treehouse. By the time I reach the top, I'm a little out of breath.

"If cancer won't do me in, this climb sure will," I quip, wiping my hands on my pants. I glance up to find Mattie, sporting the goofiest smile, holding a sign.

HOCO?

"In middle school, someone stood you up, and I did nothing about it. Now, it's our senior year, we have a minuscule amount of time together, and my mom told me you can't go to homecoming. So, this time I'm doing something," he places the sign down. "Your parents agreed to me throwing a small dance just for you in the backyard, but only if you feel up for it."

God must've crafted the most perfect best friend. "Of course, you idiot!" I exclaim, embracing him. "This is your senior year too. Why do you want to party with the 'dead'?"

Mattie shrugs. "Senior year or not, I know how little time I have left with my best friend. Kind of sucks, and I want to make the most of it. I don't care about some stupid dance, but you do. Everyone deserves to get what makes them happy; even when they're 'the dead.'"

My stomach growls, so we sit and feast. Mattie informs me we have an appointment by one, so we gobble down quickly and head out.

He's driving to keep the surprise intact. When we reach a parking lot, he covers my eyes with the same blindfold he used for Disney.

"Bucket list?" I inquire.

"Bucket list," he responds with a mix of happiness and a touch of nervousness.

We walk for what feels like an eternity, probably just two minutes, when I hear a door ding. "You may take it off now," he says, and I feel him retreat.

Inktastic.

"You don't have to, but I'm getting one and figured we could get matching. If you want to, of course," he says, shifting in his spot.

"Hmmm," I feign contemplation. Truth is, I've waited forever to get all inked up. "Depends, what do you have in mind?"

Naturally, he insists it's a surprise and urges me to trust him. At this moment, trust him I do, maybe a bit too much, as I find myself blindfolded once again, ready for our next adventure in the tattoo artist's chairs.

"I LOVE it," I exclaim, gazing at the masterpiece now residing on my upper forearm. "Why a butterfly? What is yours?"

Mattie unveils the most beautiful rose line art in the same spot as mine. "Addley Rose Mcrae, so when you are no longer with me, I know I will always have a part of you and our friendship," he says, rendering more reasons for me to shed happy tears. "The butterfly has two reasons. First, I remember when we were four; you told my mom you wanted to grow up to be a big rainbow butterfly one day. The second reason is that butterflies are signs of loved ones coming back to check on us, and butterflies love roses. So, I have my fingers crossed that you'll haunt me when you become the big rainbow butterfly you dreamed of."

By the end of his heartfelt explanation, I am a blubbering mess. "What if I want to haunt you as a worm?"

Everyone laughs, which eases some lingering sadness. Mattie had already paid beforehand, so I tip them, and we make our way out. As we head back to the car, he suddenly jerks me in the other direction.

"Okay, easy there. I'm fragile," I tease, pulling my arm away with fake pain.

"Sorry, figured I'd pick up your wrist flower thing while we are here." Mattie goes inside, leaving me to sit on the bench and enjoy the somewhat nice day. The air has become chillier since we left the house earlier. It doesn't take him more than a minute before he walks out with flowers in hand.

"Lilies are still your favorite flowers, right?" I nod, smiling.

It's the smallest things that can make someone the happiest in their darkest moments.

***

It's creeping toward six in the evening, and I've been banished upstairs until further notice, so I dive into getting ready. Mattie dubbed this our homecoming, urging me to wear the dress hanging in my closet.

The dress is a stunning red, a flowy halter style with lace and jewels that stops mid-thigh. Mom and I snagged it during the summer shopping spree, before everything took a nosedive. I opt for curled hair, slicking back the left side adorned with white pearl stick-on beads. My makeup is kept simple with a subtle champagne-colored eyeshadow and a touch of mascara, while my lips get a clear gloss.

Around seven, a knock on my door signals Dad's arrival. "Hey, princess," he opens his arms for a hug. "Your date is here."

I practically bolt down the stairs to find Mattie, decked out in a sharp black button-up, a red tie, and sleeves rolled up to flaunt his freshly tattooed arm. He looks dapper, content, and way more mature.

Our parents engage in an exhaustive photoshoot; they probably have enough pictures to fill a yearbook. Post photography, Mattie leads me to our backyard transformed into a fairy-lit haven. Mason jars dangle, flowers adorn every corner, a single table sits beside a makeshift dance floor, and a taco buffet graces a corner of the fence.

"I-Thank you so much," I hug him tight. "It's beautiful."

Mattie and I dive into the taco buffet, loading our plates, making multiple trips for seconds and thirds. Once our bellies are content, we unleash our inner dance maniacs, grooving until my lungs call for a break.

By ten, we sport matching pajamas, resetting the living room for movies and popcorn, while our parents are still out.

"I really can't thank you enough for everything tonight." And it's true. Mattie is the only one who truly respects my wishes, desires, and happiness.

Without a word, he heads out and returns five minutes later. "Almost forgot," he brandishes the cheapest, cutest, little plastic tiara. "You won homecoming queen." He gently places it on my head.

Mentally ticking Homecoming queen off my bucket list, wrapped in the cozy comfort of our teenage haven.

***

Today is the absolute highlight of October – the day I throw my epic Halloween bash. Miraculously, I managed to sweet-talk my parents into giving it a green light, a feat I'm quite proud of since I've been hosting these every year.

This time around, Mattie and I decided to spice things up by surprising each other with our costumes, ditching the usual matching routine. The guest list is tight-knit for all the right reasons, and even Jameson snagged an invite with surprisingly zero drama from Mattie. My parents are off on a cozy weekend getaway to a lake cottage, joined by Aunt May and Mr. Sinclair. Meanwhile, Ellie and Robyn are at my place, putting the finishing touches on our spooktacular transformation.

Robyn lands with a flourish from the ladder, the undisputed champion after hanging the last of the spider webs. We all take a step back to admire our Halloween masterpiece – fake webs, pumpkins, blood, and every other creepy touch you can imagine. Robyn and Ellie head to my room as I grab some water for us. With a solid two hours before the party kicks into high gear, I settle down next to Ellie on the floor, while Robyn stakes her claim at my vanity.

"How are you feeling?" Ellie asks, a genuine concern etched across her face. Truth be told, I've never felt more drained. My body is aching in places I didn't know existed, my chest is playing its own haunting melody, and fatigue is my unwelcome companion. But of course, I keep the harsh reality to myself. "Feeling great, really."

The past week has been a battle, navigating through school days as if cancer is tapping me on the shoulder, refusing to be ignored. Shoving those thoughts aside, I grab my makeup bag and spill its contents on the floor. Today's look? A simple base and eyes, maybe sprinkle in some gems for that touch of magic.

About ten minutes before the 'official' party starts, Mattie decides to make a grand entrance. "Mattie, what the heck are you wearing?" Robyn's laughter echoes through the house, and I can't resist joining in. I dash to the top of the stairs for a sneak peek.

Big.

Yellow.

Red.

"Winnie the freaking Pooh?" Laughter bursts out once again. Who dresses up as the honey-loving bear for Halloween at eighteen? "I actually love it; you're so weird though."

Hurrying back to my room, I slip into my green dress and shoes. Locking the door, I head back down, ready to dive into the adorable, slightly chaotic, and utterly memorable Halloween festivities of our high school years.

The Halloween bash kicks into high gear not long after, and after a solid three hours, the energy is starting to settle. Mattie's cozied up to my left on one couch, while Jameson and his new girlfriend Molly claim the chairs across from us. Yes, the same Molly he cheated with. Oddly enough, it's all water under the bridge now. Why cling to a grudge over something so trivial, especially when you know the end of the story?

"I like your costume. Tinker Bell was my second crush," Mattie whispers into my ear, his tone carrying a playful undertone.

I've known that for ages; he's never spilled the beans on his first crush. I've asked countless times, thrown out numerous guesses, but he always slyly evades the question, mentioning only that she was in his kindergarten class. Whatever it is, it's buried in the past, and I'm okay not knowing. Perhaps he's just a tad embarrassed or something.

Surveying the room, I realize that most of the guests have either departed or are in the process of doing so. Somewhere in the midst of conversation, I rest my head on Mattie's shoulder, gradually succumbing to the sweet lull of sleep. The next morning, I woke up in my bed, neatly tucked in.

Venturing downstairs, the place is eerily spotless, a testament to Mattie's legendary cleanup skills. And, of course, in true Mattie fashion, there's a note waiting for me.

> *Party was great, hope you slept well. Dont worry about the mess, Ellison and I got it.*
>
> *-Mattie*

November

The chill in the air has deepened significantly this past week, prompting Mom to declare today a soup and movie day. We're currently en route to the store, having combined the outing with my appointment.

Same news.

No news.

Whether it's the biting cold or the relentless grip of cancer, my bones feel unnervingly fragile. It's as if applying even the slightest pressure would shatter them into a million delicate pieces.

The frigid air intensifies my breathing struggles, leading Dr. Karas to suggest checking into the cancer ward until the end. I staunchly refused, asserting that I won't spend my remaining time confined to a hospital bed. Dr. Karas, in turn, advised Mom that the optimal solution is to sleep with a specialized mask and prescribed an inhaler to ease my respiratory struggles.

Paxton is en route home, with his plane scheduled to land at five, leaving us with a few hours to spare. I hastily exit the car upon arrival, making a beeline for the restroom

Another occurrence that's become all too frequent—rushing somewhere to rid myself of the persistent nausea. After finding relief, I tidy up and rendezvous with Mom in the cracker aisle. She's already amassed the ingredients for my favorite, chicken and dumplings.

We continue our meandering journey through the store for another fifteen minutes when my phone chimes.

A text from Paxton.

<u>Sorry, don't think I can make it for Thanksgiving</u>

"Mom, I need to sit. Keys, please." I snatch them from her, muttering a hasty sorry before storming out the door. I promptly dial his number, the frustration mounting with each unanswered call. It takes four attempts before he finally picks up.

"Sis, I'm sor—" I don't allow him to finish.

"I am sick of hearing that word. You aren't sorry. Unless you mean you're a sorry excuse of a sibling. This was important. We need you here. I need you here, but you wouldn't know because all I get is a two-word text once a month." Tears cascade down my cheeks. "Paxton, you have no idea what is going on. You're too scared to face Mom and Dad, and you've pushed me away too." My breathing becomes ragged.

Paxton sighs on the other side of the line. "I don't know what you want from me, Addley."

"I want my brother to be my brother again while he still can." With that, I hang up and power off my phone.

***

Paxton and I schemed up a prank to play on Kenny when she returned from the store with Mom. The twins had been engaged in a fierce prank war for the past week. I had just finished securing the bucket when the car's headlights peeked through the trees. Hiding with Paxton in the bushes, we anxiously waited for Kenny to approach and open the door. It wasn't until it was too late that I realized Mom was the one carrying the groceries to the door. Before I could intervene, Mom was drenched in red paint, reminiscent of Carrie.

"PAXTON JOEL MCRAE!" Steam practically poured from her ears. Paxton started to stand up and approach her, but I pulled him back down and hurried out.

"Sorry, Mom. Paxton didn't do this. I just wanted to be part of the fun." I handed Mom the waiting towel.

She shook her head and sighed. "Tomorrow is Thanksgiving; we will discuss punishment after." She started walking toward the backyard, mumbling something.

"Don't tell Kenny, but you're my favorite sister," Paxton said, suddenly at my side.

"You owe me for eternity."

I ended up grounded for three weeks after that escapade.

***

As I open my eyes, I find myself lying on the couch. I must have dozed off, and Dad brought me here. My phone rests on the coffee table, so I grab it, hoping for a call or text from Paxton. Disappointment sets in when I see nothing.

I toss my phone onto the couch and decide to take a quick bath. As I step out, I catch a glimpse of myself in the mirror. It's been a while since I've really looked at myself. The toll of constant vomiting and minimal eating is evident. My cheeks, once the fullest part of my face, are now the only plump feature.

Dark circles under my eyes tell tales of sleepless nights. Winter layers conceal more than just the cold; they hide the changes in my appearance. I throw a blanket over the mirror, get dressed in sweats, and head downstairs to the empty kitchen. A note from Mom states they won't be back until tomorrow.

Loneliness creeps in—funny, but not really. Six months ago, the idea of being alone excited me. Graduating meant freedom from answering to anyone. Now, solitude feels suffocating. I considered texting Mattie, but he's been occupied. Ellison and Robyn are away at colleges. Jameson is at the lake with his family.

I grab a bowl of chicken soup and retreat to my room. Tray in hand, I settle into bed, turning on the Hallmark channel, hoping the Christmas movie might lift my spirits. However, neither food nor movies appeal to me, so I find myself scrolling through my phone, confronted by the seemingly endless happiness of my classmates. Envy takes hold.

A secret gnaws at me—I've been questioning my choices. Wondering if not trying was better than trying and failing. I joined an online group for terminal cancer patients, hoping for solace, but it only deepened my despair.

Lately, thoughts of ending it all have crossed my mind. Putting everyone, including myself, out of their misery. Death is inevitable, and the waiting becomes unbearable. It's not the dying part that scares me; it's the uncertainty of when. Every doctor's estimate is just that—an estimate. Nobody knows when, except maybe me.

***

"I'm thankful for the years I got with Kenny." The words hang heavy in the air as we go around the table, expressing gratitude for this year. It's been three long months since Kenny left. Paxton immerses himself in school, Dad piles on extra shifts, and Mom refuses to give me space.

Yet, we are all hurting.

"Okay, let's just say grace," Mom motions for us to join hands, deflecting any mention of her name.

Still, we are all hurting.

I excuse myself halfway through dinner, retreating to my room. Jameson had to join his parents at his dad's family gathering, which is a letdown, but thankfully, Mattie is here.

In the silence that follows, the weight of Kenny's absence fills the room, a metaphorical void that no words or prayers can truly fill.

***

I toss and turn throughout the night, the exhaustion of my body contrasting with the restlessness of my mind. Sleep eludes me, and every time I close my eyes, Kenny's presence haunts me.

Waiting for me.

How morbid it all sounds.

After an hour of staring at the wall in the darkness, I surrender to the wakefulness and decide to get up. Downstairs, I hear the murmur of Mom and Dad's conversation. Dad is lugging in groceries, and Mom is immersed in preparing food for tomorrow. As I enter the kitchen, I discover Paxton wearing an apron, chopping vegetables while Mom tends to the turkey.

"It's about time you woke up," Paxton remarks with a hint of attitude. I'm still upset with him, but I realize he doesn't know the whole story and didn't want to come this week.

I shrug my shoulders as I grab the orange juice from the fridge and pour it into a glass. Paxton gestures to Mom, prompting her to leave the kitchen. He pulls out a chair for me at the table.

"We need to talk," he tells me as I take my seat.

You have no idea, I think to myself but respond with a simple, "Okay."

To be honest, I didn't pay much attention to whatever he said because at some point, exhaustion claimed me, and I drifted into an uneasy slumber.

I wake up on the couch around three in the afternoon, and I'm pretty sure Dad must've moved me here. My phone's lying on the coffee table, and I grab it, hoping to find a call or text from Paxton. Nothing. I toss the phone back on the couch and decide to take a quick bath.

As I stare at myself in the mirror, I realize I haven't really looked at myself lately. The constant vomiting and lack of eating have taken a toll. My cheeks are the only chunky part left. Dark circles under my eyes show nights of little sleep. I drape the blanket back over the mirror and throw on a pair of sweats before heading downstairs.

Mom left a note saying they won't be back until tomorrow. It's just me.

Lonely

Lonely

Lonely

It's funny how, six months ago, I was all about the freedom of graduating and being on my own. Now, being home alone feels depressing. I've tried reaching out to Mattie, Ellison, and Robyn, but everyone seems too busy. Friends are away, and seeing their happy posts on social media makes me envy their carefree moments.

Secretly, I've been wondering if my decision not to try was the right one. The waiting game is getting to me. I joined an online group for terminal cancer patients, hoping to find some comfort, but it's only making me more depressed. Thoughts of ending it all have crossed my mind.

The Christmas movie on the Hallmark channel doesn't do anything for me. I envy the happy faces on my phone. In the silence of my room, the weight of my choices hangs heavy. The loneliness turns into a storm, and I'm caught in its turbulent emotions.

The next day, Mom sticks me on couch duty, snapping at me whenever I try to help. Paxton's giving me the cold shoulder, making me second-guess sharing the mess that's become my life. It's not like he's treating me amazing, but compared to the rest, it's a freakin' oasis of normal.

I call Paxton in when the parade kicks off, hoping for some bonding time. He responds with a dose of bitterness, shutting me down. The next hours are a family reunion with a side of Paxton's icy vibes. On the flip side, Mattie and Aunt May bring a bit of relief, even though Paxton's still in the dark about my secret turmoil.

Dinner is announced, and we gather around a meticulously set table. Mom went all out, aiming for the best last Thanksgiving. During the 'what we're thankful for' round, Paxton throws shade my way. He's grateful for being dragged here to feel unwelcome, and he singles me out as the one who made him feel welcome after Kenny's death.

In response, I stood up, locking eyes with him. "I'm thankful this is my last Thanksgiving."

It hits hard. Paxton erupts, yelling at me not to joke about it. I just shrug, walking out. "Wasn't a joke." I drive off, no destination in mind, just craving the open road to drown out the mess inside my head.

***

"Addley, don't tell Mom and Dad. Please, I am begging." I toss Kenny onto my bed. She stumbled in after a party with the jocks, wasted beyond humor. I exit the room, grabbing a bottle of water and two ibuprofen from our bathroom.

"Take these. I read somewhere that you need to stay on top of it so you're not hungover as bad." I extend everything towards her. "And, of course not. You would get into serious trouble, and then you won't be able to take me to the concert on Friday."

***

I find myself driving to the graveyard. You'd think three years would be enough healing time, right? Movies always make it seem that way, but real life is so different. The grief isn't some linear path; it's a tangled mess of emotions.

"God, I miss you so damn much." Here come the tears. "I can't handle this anymore, Ken. It's like a constant ache. I'm not ready to die, but..." Deep breaths. Get it out now. Maybe it'll help, or maybe I'm just talking to the wind. "Lately, I've thought about ending it. Just to stop the pain, you know? I've even written a note."

Rubbing the snot on the back of my sleeve, I continue. "I want to do it. The waiting game is terrifying. Doctors yap about the troubles of cancer, but no one warns you about this existential dread. Knowing any moment I could just crumble and die has given me the worst anxiety. I've even looked into assisted suicide, but there's no way Mom and Dad would ever get on board with that."

Sticks snap behind me, leaves rustle, and I hear someone sniffling. "I didn't know," Paxton whispers before wrapping his arms around me. "I should've been there for you more."

We sit there as I spill my guts. "I'm not going to end it. It's just so damn scary."

"I know you wouldn't, but maybe you should talk to someone. You have everyone, but sometimes we're just not enough in that way."

He's right, and maybe it's time I stop being so stubborn. "Monday, I'll call the doctor for recommendations." Paxton grabs my hand, pulling me up. We hop into his car, and he drives off. "I'm sorry I dozed off." I manage a weak smile.

"I'm sorry for flipping out over something so dumb."

"It was pretty childish, I'll admit."

We head back home to grab some food and retreat to his room for a movie and some sibling time.

I'm going to miss this.

I'm going to miss him.

Chapter Seven

December

One week 'til winter break, and I'm drowning. The frigid air is messing with my lungs, making the inhaler my new BFF. Paxton's doing the homeschooling thing, joining forces with Mattie whenever they're not glued together. Ellie and I, trudging to our last class, map out our break plans. She's off to ski in Colorado with Robyn, and me? I'm practically planning a hibernation fest in my bed for two weeks.

Always exhausted. Haven't spilled the beans to Mom, but thinking of ditching school next semester. I'll miss the classroom vibe, but sunrise struggles? Nah, not for me.

"Still on for studying later? Totally get it if you're not feeling it," Ellie interrupts my thoughts.

I nod, our paths diverging. European history's dragging its feet like it's auditioning for a slow-motion movie. Mr. Benton drops midterm bombshells as we shuffle out. "Sheet filled out by Thursday." Great.

***

Mom's hyped when I announce the study sesh at our place. Snacks, drinks, desserts – she's on it. Robyn's on my case about question eight. Predicting an epic fail, as usual. A secret sleepover? Seemed like a good idea. Now, regret's my middle name. Haven't slept, been besties with the toilet, throwing up my guts.

"Addie, you good?" Mattie whispers, barging in.

I try pushing him away, "Back to bed. I'm a pro at this." Sleepy smiles and feeble attempts to kick him out fail as the vomiting encore begins. Mattie's the hair-holder, the back-rubber. "You're okay," he repeats. I laugh, it's not funny. "No, I'm not." Sleep's a myth. "Go back to bed, please. School's in two hours."

He's stubborn, "We promised best friends until the end, remember? I'm not bailing now." Side by side, the ticking clock mocks our wasted time.

***

Friday's here, midterms done. Auditorium's playing holiday flicks, and the gym's buzzing. Principal summons me to Mr. Castee's room. As if a slip could change my world.

Senior's hall, a knock, and I'm in. Concern fills Mr. Castee's eyes, pointing out the bruises and weight loss. Pity or not, confessing my struggles isn't an option. "Thanks, but no dark secrets here," I retorted, throwing shade. Grab my purse, door slam – end of that.

***

Mattie's a ticking bomb post my Mr. Castee showdown. "You could've walked away," he sighs.

"Should've, yeah," my head meets the cold window. Taking the scenic route, snow starts falling. "Pull over, please." It's my last first snowfall – warmth in a cold world. Silent snow, warm car, and apologies hang in the air.

"I'm sorry," I start.

"No need," he mumbles, eyes down.

"No, Mattie. I'm a mess. I've been selfish, mad, and it sucks." Angry tears spill, his silence cuts deep.

"You don't think I get it?" he finally says. "I see you, stressed over senior year. You're pushing everyone away. Struggling alone. Dying on your terms. I've backed off, but no more." "Okay."

***

Called Mom, snowplay's over, and the truth stings.

"I'll still cheer you on. Snow angel or not, I've got your back. I'm not ready to lose my best friend, Addley," Mattie says, wiping away a tear.

Feels like the last chapter of a book, and I'm not ready for the ending.

***

Dragged Paxton out for last-minute Christmas shopping on Christmas Eve. Brilliant, right? He's not convinced.

"Why wait? Online shopping is a thing, you know," he groans.

"But it's the most wonderful time of the year! Online's for losers," I fire back, marching toward the food court. Dump my bags on the table while Paxton grabs food. He offers, I decline, and he returns with sushi and soup. A grateful smile, and we dive into the Christmas chaos.

Pax's been on duty, hovering like a protective eagle. Took Kenny's old room next to mine, ready to swoop in. So far, no swooping needed. Appreciate the effort, but he's bordering on Mom and Dad level. Refuses to let me be a lone wolf, except in the bathroom.

Driving's a challenge with pain and nausea, took ages to persuade him to drive, citing 'germs' and 'walking' drama. Sip soup, wait for Paxton to finish, then hit a few more shops.

Finally, I banished him to the car for his gift.

I offered to help carry bags, he insists on shouldering it all. Third floor, end of the mall - my destination clear, gift idea locked in.

***

Christmas Eve at the Sinclairs' – a tradition etched in memory. The hustle in the kitchen, dads in the family room, and the gang chilling in the now Mattie-claimed basement, minus Kenny.

While the guys dive into a new game, I retreat to Mattie's old room. His hammock chair invites me by the window to read and witness the snowfall – pure magic. The world is slow-motion, silent, and serene.

A tap on my shoulder interrupts the trance. "Dinner's almost ready, kiddo." Dad offers a hand, and we head to the dining room. The table's set, Mattie between Paxton and me. Prayer kicks off dinner, and conversations about school, work, and college fill the air. The unspoken truth: Stanford's a no-go, my secret application hidden from the world.

Food sits on my plate, untouched. Aunt May sends me to the couch, where The Polar Express awaits. The boys join midway, and after the movie, I decide to head home, exhausted but grateful.

Back at my place, Mattie senses my fatigue and offers help. I accept – a promise kept. Upstairs, he checks if I need anything, and with laughter, popcorn, and matching PJs, our Christmas Eve sleepover begins, just like old times.

In my bathroom, hot water soothes, but a leg gives way, and chaos ensues. Wet floors, a ripped curtain, and Mattie tripping over. Laughter conquers pain, and for a moment, tomorrow's worries fade. It's a scene straight out of the movies.

"Are you okay?" he asks amid laughter. "What happened?"

"The shower and I had a big misunderstanding." Laughter echoes, drowning out every worry, just like a perfect Christmas Eve should be.

Christmas morning, my last one. The excitement is real.

"Santa came!" I shake Mattie, trying to drag him into my festive energy.

"You're such a child. Five more minutes, please," he groans, hiding under the pillow.

"I have a feeling Santa brought some awesome presents. I could very much be wrong."

"Get up," smack, "Get up," smack, "Get u-"

"I'M UP!" Mattie's at the foot of the bed now. "Didn't you hear? Santa came. Get *your* lazy butt up."

The audacity.

We head to the bathroom together. Mattie, sensing I'm not at my best, offers a piggyback ride. A small promise kept, but a promise nonetheless.

Reaching the kitchen, we go for our traditional matching cereal and bowl sets. Paxton throws a comment about our breakfast choices.

"You're so gross," he says as I grab the Raisin Bran set.

"It's the best, and you have no room to talk with your Wheat Thins," I retorted. "Now, that's what I call disgusting."

Cereal banter continues as Mattie and Paxton dive into game talk. I move to the living room, open the blinds, start up the fireplace, and cozy up with a book.

White Christmases are the best. The cold and the snow, the silent blizzard – pure joy.

Knock Knock Knock.

Aunt May and Mr. Sinclair enter, still in their boring normal pajamas.

"It's Christmas, Aunt May! What are you wearing?" I tease. "Not surprised, though, so I got you two something." Mattie brings in their sets. "Just this once, and I will love you forever."

Aunt May holds back tears, and Mr. Sinclair, usually stoic, hides a frown and a single tear before walking away. Christmas, with its joys and subtle sadness, wraps us in its bittersweet embrace.

***

"Open mine next," Mattie hands Paxton the worst-wrapped present ever, a masterpiece in terrible wrapping. Inside are tickets to some concert.

Mattie finds it amusing to wrap gifts in the most terrible ways. One year, my gifts were wrapped in white printer paper with barely any tape. Most of the time, it looks like he just crumples the wrapping into a ball and puts tape on it. As much as I appreciate a beautiful wrapping job, his gifts wouldn't feel the same without it.

We've been going around, opening gifts for nearly an hour.

"Okay, I wasn't sure what to get everyone this year, so I hope these will do." I hand everyone their own bag with similar items, almost. "It's simple, but I hope you love them." Their favorite snacks, movies, gift cards, etcetera.

I told everyone that I truly did not want any presents this year, for obvious reasons, of course.

Nobody listened.

Mom and Dad bought me comfortable clothes and slippers, Paxton got me some books, and the Sinclairs and my parents decided a week trip to the mountains would be nice for me, so they gifted that to me.

"Thank you, guys, for everything. I love you all." The love wrapped in those imperfectly wrapped gifts speaks louder than any ribbon or bow could convey.

***

Christmas is almost over, and Mattie and I still haven't exchanged gifts. The parents and Paxton are playing games in the dining room, and the two of us are in the family room, watching movies and sipping hot cocoa.

"I got you something. Want to know what it is?" He hands me a small box wrapped hideously.

The box holds the cutest handmade friendship bracelet that I can tell he put time into. "It's so adorable. I love it! Thank you, Mattie," I wrap my arm around his side and give him a hug.

"You wanted simple, and I know you like the sentimental homemade stuff," he shrugs it off like it's nothing.

"My turn. Can you get the box from under my bed, please? No peeking." Mattie nods his head and makes his way upstairs, coming back not even thirty seconds later.

"This isn't a track; you didn't have to sprint," I joke. "Go ahead; you may peek now."

Mattie slowly opens the box and pulls everything out, taking a nice long look at everything.

"I love it," he breathes out when he's finished. A picture of us printed on a hoodie, like before but updated, a new soccer ball, and Sprinkles the fish.

"After our talk the other day, I figured I could maybe help ease some of the pain. Now you know you will always have your number one fan with you no matter what." I smiled at him. "Press the fin."

Mattie does as I say and presses the button for the message I had put in.

> *"Hi Matthew Sinclair. I bet you're winning all your games and doing great in life. You are the best friend anyone could ever ask for. I hope you remember to put yourself out there because I know how lame you can be. I hope you are living the*

> *life you always dreamed of. I hope you know I am still your number one fan cheering you on. I love you, Mattie."*

The sound of Mattie's sniffling draws my attention back to him. "I didn't mean to upset you. I'm sorry."

Mattie just shakes his head before wiping the few tears left. "No, I love this. Thank you, Addie, thank you so much." The warmth of the moment, mixed with gratitude, fills the room as Christmas draws to a close, leaving a bittersweet memory behind.

***

New Year's Eve, and I am stuck at home with the parents. I say stuck, but not because of them; I haven't felt the best today. The aches have gotten significantly worse over the past two or however many days. Convincing Paxton to go hang out with his old high school friends was hard, but somehow I managed to.

I'm forcing myself to stay awake so I can watch the ball drop. Only ten minutes left, I think I can do that. Mattie dropped by an hour ago and has been playing board games with everyone until now.

"I have an idea, and before you say no, hear me out." Mattie pulls out a can from his hoodie pocket. "I know you aren't feeling well, but New Year's seems like a perfect time to mark another thing off the list." Reluctantly, I grab the can of some fruity-flavored alcoholic drink from him.

I have never had any alcohol ever. I swore it off since everything with Kenny. Alcohol leads to bad things, and I never wanted to put myself in that position, but since my diagnosis, I figured what's the harm in finding out what the fuss is about.

"Cheers." We clink the cans, and I take a sip. "Not bad, I guess." I take another tiny drink. It's mango or something.

"One-minute countdown is starting!" Dad yells up from the stairs. The more I try, the more I think it is disgusting; it just tastes like flavored sparkling water with a bit of rubbing alcohol.

I hear our parents talking about their kiss, ew, and decide Mattie could be my New Year's kiss this year. "Hey Mattie, let me kiss you." I laugh a little, feeling a tad awkward.

"Okay, you weirdo, if that's what you want."

The countdown starts.

10

He makes his way over and sits next to me.

9

8

7

6

5

4

I look over at him and contemplate if this is a good idea.

3

2

We lean into each other

1

Chapter Eight

January

And I empty my stomach all over him.

"Oh my gosh, I am so sorry, Mattie. Seriously, did that just happen?" I keep apologizing as we shuffle our way to the bathroom.

"Bucket list item unlocked, and you could use a rinse." He gently plops me down on the bathroom floor. "Need a hand?"

My eyes go wide.

"Nah, I can fetch your mom or someone. Definitely not me helping you. Not unless you want me to, and if you do, I mean, I guess I could, but..." He stumbles over his words, and it's almost adorable.

"I think I'll manage. Go hit the shower." I wave him away. After a moment, he finally retreats. I crank the water to mostly hot, toss in some bath salts and bubbles, and prepare for the post-vomit spa.

As the tub fills with bubbles, I lower myself in, feeling the warmth seep into every ache in my body. My slender physique.

I had a heart-to-heart with my folks the other day, agreeing to take a break from school. The daily grind is just too much, especially since the weirdness has become glaringly obvious in the past week alone.

I've concluded that attending school every single day isn't worth it, especially now that it's becoming clear that something's off.

After a good scrub, I hop out, run a brush through my thinning hair, and scrub my teeth till the nasty taste is gone. Then, I throw on some pajamas and head to my closet.

By the time I finish, Mattie's already snoozing in the chair. A glass of water and my vitamins stand beside the bed—his thoughtful touch.

"Goodnight, Matthew," I whisper, tucking him in and snuffing out the fireplace. The night might not have gone as planned, but hey, at least we managed to spice up the bucket list with some unexpected drama.

***

Monday, the dreaded comeback of the school saga. Mom was practically over the moon when I declared my escape from the halls of academia. Her excitement dampened a bit when I dropped the bomb that I still plan on finishing. She sees it as a "what's the point" scenario, which, yeah, I get it. But, come on, I've put in the hours. Silly? Maybe, but it's silly.

Ellie swoops in right after her airport departure, probably in need of a break from family drama. We dive into break updates, and she spills about getting accepted into some fashion school in Europe. Seriously, the girl is killing it, and I can't help but be genuinely thrilled for her.

I shrug, flipping over in the recliner. "Some days are worse. Today's not too bad." The past week has seen me camping out in the living room; tackling the stairs feels like scaling Mount Everest. Walking, in general, leaves me gasping for air like I'm competing for an Olympic gold in breathlessness.

"In a few days, I've got an appointment. Dad's all about getting me on some depression meds," I roll my eyes for dramatic effect. "You'd think he'd get it by now, right? It's a gloomy situation, but I'm not depressed, and I sure as heck won't be popping that stuff."

Dad had me on antidepressants when Kenny checked out. They didn't magically fix everything; instead, they just made me contemplate joining Kenny on the other side. A weird side effect for meds supposedly designed to prevent that kind of thing.

***

Ellie jetted out a few hours ago. Mom and Dad are off to some charity auction, Paxton is in his own galaxy, and I'm in desperate need of a shower. Ever since the New Year's incident, discovering those ugly, dark bruises, Mom's been on duty helping me shower when I'm not up for it.

Caught snippets of Mom and Dad's hush-hush discussion about hiring a nurse to bring the TLC to my doorstep. They see the same shadows I do.

My body's staging a protest, my oxygen supply is staging a walkout, and I'm shedding pounds faster than you can say "teen metabolism."

Downhill.

Rapid descent.

The docs painted a hopeful picture with a one-year estimate, but we all know cancer's got a need for speed, and it's not a patient passenger.

Guess I'll catch a quick nap until Mom swoops in to assist me again.

***

Woke up to a door-shaking serenade at midnight, accompanied by a symphony of jingling keys.

"Addie!" Mattie's voice echoes through the front door. He storms in, shutting the door with a theatrical flair. "Why didn't you answer your phone?"

I rub the sleep from my eyes, letting out a yawn. "I was asleep," I mutter, grabbing my phone. "Guess it's dead. What's up?"

Mattie, in full disapproval mode, shakes his head and starts shedding his coat and shoes. "Your parents called mine since you weren't answering. They got caught in the snowstorm, so they're hotel-bound tonight."

Fantastic. Now, I'll have to endure the lingering grossness a bit longer.

"Thanks for letting me know, and sorry for not answering."

"I get that you're sorry, but, Addley, you can't be doing that. You need to make sure your phone is charged and on at all times. What if—" He pauses, glancing down at his feet. "I was scared to come over here. Scared thinking I would walk through the doors and find you lifeless," he whispers, barely audible.

"I get it, Mattie, but my phone was dead, and I was asleep. Nothing was wrong. I'm alive. I spend more time pondering my last breath than my phone's battery. Excuse me." I don't love my tone, but he needs to understand this isn't a big deal. "You were worried I'd be dead, and that's awful, but I'm constantly wondering when my last breath will be. So instead of wasting time arguing over what I should have done, can we just move on?"

I can't see it, but I'm pretty sure he rolled his eyes.

"Fine."

After whatever tension danced its way out, I made Mattie stand on the other side of the door as I indulged in a makeshift sponge bath before settling into the living room with a movie. Falling back asleep didn't take long.

***

All my friends are out there, living their best lives, while I'm stuck at home playing nurse roulette with Nurse Lindsay.

Doctor Karas delivered an extensive briefing on the impending steps my parents and I need to take when the curtain eventually falls. It's like, just when I start to get comfortable and wrap my head around my impending expiration date, reality slaps me back to the harsh truth.

Don't get me wrong, I'm not ready to punch out before punching in for a full, kick-ass life. I just didn't realize how hard it would hit me. But I've got to be the brave one, right? The one making sure everyone else is holding it together when my time comes.

I used to think I was scared of dying, and yeah, maybe I am, but more than anything, I'm terrified of disappointing and hurting the people I love. Sometimes my mind wanders into the what-ifs.

What if I took better care of myself?

What if I went for check-ups sooner?

What if I kicked chemo into gear when the doctor first dropped the "C" bomb?

So many what-ifs, and not a single one I can change now. Cue the waterworks, chest tightening, full-blown panic attack. Lindsay swoops in, guiding me through her magical calming exercises.

Find colors in the room.

Numbers.

Smells.

And, after a bit of struggle, I can breathe again. Kind of.

"Thanks," I murmur as she hands me a glass of water and what I assume are my anxiety pills. While I said no to antidepressants, I caved on something to tackle the rabbit hole. "Really, I know it's your job to help me, but I appreciate you."

***

As the end of the month looms, my days blur into a repetitive loop of sleep, eat, vomit, repeat. Occasionally, a fleeting burst of energy lasts for no more than three hours, only to be followed by a plunge into a bottomless abyss.

Amidst the monotony of nausea, a glimmer of bittersweet news emerges. Mattie receives his golden ticket – the acceptance letter from the University of Michigan and a full-ride soccer scholarship. I'm drowning in pride for him, even as my own world crumbles.

Paxton saunters into the kitchen. "Mom said you needed my help with something."

"I need help surprising Mattie. Just a little dinner thing or whatever to celebrate."

Paxton raises an eyebrow. "Isn't that usually what a graduation party is for?"

Fingers idly pick at the skin around my nails as I search for the right words. "Which I won't be able to attend."

Understanding dawns on his face. "What do you need me to do?"

So, I text Mattie to come over after school, and Paxton and I embark on a half-hearted attempt at celebration, decorating the dining room with lackluster yellow and blue balloons. We half-heartedly bake a cake in the shape of a thirteen, Mattie's jersey number. The day is a half-hearted whirlwind of preparations.

"It's something," I mutter. "Thank you." I raise my arms for a hug. "Please go shower; you stink."

"You stink worse." Paxton forces a laugh before heading upstairs.

An hour later, Aunt May and Mr. Sinclair arrive, and another thirty minutes pass before Mattie walks through the door.

"What is this, Addie?" he asks with a half-hearted smile, not as half-hearted as mine.

"Congratulations, you're going to be a soccer star." I stand up, but the excitement in my eyes barely reaches my lips. I give him a half-hearted hug. "I can't wait to cheer you on." I mumble in his ear before stepping back.

Our families head to the dining room, where the table is adorned with the uninspired culinary creations Paxton and I half-heartedly whipped up.

The evening unfolds with forced smiles and subdued laughter. No worries about the uncertain future, just a palpable undercurrent of sadness lingering beneath the facade of celebration.

Chapter Nine

February

As I pick up Robyn's FaceTime call, she's practically bubbling with excitement, "Hey! Ellie and I were thinking of throwing the most adorable Galentine's sleepover ever this year. What do you think? You in? Of course, no pressure. But seriously, it's going to be cuteness overload!"

A few weeks back, I spilled the beans to her about my health, and we had a heart-to-heart. Tears were shed, but it was a necessary talk. Initially, Robyn was a tad miffed about being out of the loop, but she quickly brushed it off. She realized that spending time being upset would take away the precious moments we have left.

"Absolutely! I'll give Mom the heads up, so she can raid the store for the cutest sleepover snacks. How about around six? Bring on the cute vibes!"

We chat excitedly until Robyn has to head to class as her lunch break ends. Today has been super heartwarming, probably the best I've felt in ages. Of course, with the good comes the not-so-great, so I've been taking things slow and steady.

I shoot a quick text to Mom, getting the green light for the girls to come over. Nurse Lindsay, my trusty sidekick, assists me with a shower—well, she stands guard on the other side of the door, just in case. Having Nurse Lindsay around makes Mom worry less about providing the right help in certain situations.

As the clock ticks closer to Robyn and Ellie's arrival, Mom walks in with bags of groceries. "Hope you're okay with us ordering wings and pizza. Lost track of time," she says, wrestling with the door.

"No worries, Mom! Thanks a bunch." I give her a quick hug before attempting to help with the groceries. Mom, in true mom fashion, swats me away with a smile, saying, "Go rest, sweetheart." I roll my eyes, but she doesn't stop me.

A few minutes later, the doorbell chimes, signaling the arrival of Robyn and Ellie. Robyn clutches a stash of adorable candies and chocolates, while Ellie presents two movies with a grin. "The Notebook or Midnight Sun?"

After a night filled with laughter and tears (courtesy of a tearjerker movie), Robyn remarks on the ending. Her eyes widen, and she turns to me, "Oh, shoot, I'm so sorry! That was insensitive—"

I cut her off, "No need to apologize, Robs. We're all good." Life and death are like two peas in a pod, but it doesn't make the idea of saying goodbye any easier.

Later that night, I find myself snuggling up to the trash can, having had a wild nightmare about my own funeral. Not gory, just super vivid, like I was already in ghost mode, watching the scene unfold. As the sun slowly rises, I finally close my eyes, letting the sweet embrace of sleep take over.

***

As I stir from my slumber, I find Robyn and Ellie on the other couch, diligently cleaning up the room.

They're engrossed in some reality show, and I can't help but smile.

"Hey, morning, you two," I greet them, rubbing the last remnants of sleep from my eyes. "What's the time anyway?"

Robyn shrugs, "It could be two in the afternoon. You seemed so peaceful, and we didn't want to disturb you." She pauses the show and adds, "Oh, by the way, this got delivered about an hour ago."

She hands me an envelope, and I eagerly tear it open.

Lo and behold, it's a note from Mattie.

If youre feeling up to it

please be ready by five

-Mattie

Inside the manila envelope, I discover a neatly folded blindfold and a handful of nausea suckers. Robyn, Ellie, and I decide to make the most of our time together by ordering some delicious Mexican food through DoorDash and indulging ourselves before they have to head home.

As the clock ticks closer to the time to meet Mattie, I grab my phone and shoot him a text.

Addley: Hey what should I wear?

Mattie: Probably something to keep you warm

Mattie: Ready to mark off another bucket list item?

Addley: Always

Mattie: I am going to shower. See you in a bit. Don't forget the blindfold!

Addley: Love you, Mattie.

Shoving my phone aside, I sluggishly roll my way into the downstairs bedroom, the guest room turned into a gloomy sanctuary. Mom and Dad seem to be preparing it for some inevitable, grim eventuality.

Most of my comfort clothes have been banished here. Grabbing a pair of yoga pants, fluffy socks, and an oversized long-sleeved shirt, I dress in haste. Glancing at the clock, there's still half an hour before I need to face the world. I slump onto the bed, seeking solace in the company of Sprinkles.

Suddenly, I'm roused from my drowsy escape. "Addley... Addley... wakey wakey... Addie, wake up." Mattie's voice barely penetrates my consciousness.

"I'm awake, let me be." My voice is a raspy murmur. "Oh no, I fell asleep. Did I ruin the plans?"

Mattie chuckles, shaking his head. "It's only ten minutes later. You don't have to go; we can do this another time." He trails off, glancing at the unsightly fish in my grasp. "Sprinkles found his way downstairs."

"Caught Mom trying to toss it out." Maybe she didn't understand how much I cherished this tattered thing, but I'll give her credit; it was barely holding on.

Dragging myself out of bed, Mattie assists me into my wheelchair.

"You can go back to sleep if you want, and we can do this another day." Mattie halts, pivoting me to face him. "We don't have to finish your list."

"I know that, but I'm kind of looking forward to it," I reply, heading for the front door. "You coming, or what?"

Mattie skillfully maneuvered his truck into a parking spot after a grueling fifteen-minute drive. As I fumbled to retrieve the black blindfold from my pocket, he intervened, his voice cutting through the silence. "You don't actually have to wear it, Addley."

I nonchalantly shrugged. "It's a tradition at this point." With that, I draped the cloth over my eyes. "Okay, I'm ready."

He guided me out and steered me toward what seemed to be a door, but suddenly, the unmistakable scent of chlorine hit me like a wave.

"No," I whispered, disbelieving. "Matthew Sinclair, **YOU** added this to my list."

He chuckled, his response laden with mischief. "Live a little."

"No peeking," I playfully wagged my finger at him, the angst in my tone muted by the whirlwind of teenage emotions.

***

I'm shivering like a wet cat as we cruise back home, but not in style—in the back of a cop car.

"I can't believe you talked me into that."

"I can't believe you pulled the cancer card," Mattie howls with laughter.

You see, Mattie forgot to check for guards while we were having our splashy escapade. The guards heard, and bam! Next thing you know, we're getting a royal escort back home.

The cancer card worked its magic, though. Instead of being hauled off to the station, Officer Cayman chauffeured us straight to my driveway. Mom, Dad, and May are already waiting outside.

God, I'm begging you, just end it now. I'd rather meet my demise than have to explain to them the aquatic misadventure that landed us in the backseat of a police cruiser.

"Remind me again why the two of you were caught, naked, in the community pool?" Mom is fuming, while May and Dad are in the living room practically rolling on the floor with laughter.

"I'd rather die than talk about this. I just want to take a hot bath and go to bed. Please, Mom." Even though Officer Cayman spoke with her, and Mattie and I have explained for the past hour, she just keeps asking.

"Bucket list item," I shoot dagger eyes over to my partner in aquatic crime. "One that I didn't put on there."

Mattie puts his hands up in defense. "I did not make you, though."

I roll my eyes. "Whatever, Mom, it could have been worse. Let me go now. Goodnight, I love you."

I make my way to the living room. "Stop laughing. It's rude." Obviously, that only makes them laugh even more, and at this point, I'm laughing too

"Fine, it's a little funny. Just a little."

The snow has formed a cozy blanket over the yard. School was let out early due to the roads, so I find myself in Mattie's room, conquering the virtual battlefield in Call of Duty. I suspect he's letting me win.

"Okay, I can't play anymore. My eyes hurt from staring at the TV for so long." He sets his controller down. "You need anything from the kitchen?"

I nod and hop into his recliner. "Hot chocolate, please."

Mattie makes his way upstairs as I get comfy. Pulling a blanket over me, I grab the book I've been reading off the nightstand and flip to the bookmarked page. Mattie refills my mug countless times as I lose myself in my book, page after page. I'm so absorbed that I only notice his soft snores when it's barely nine at night.

I put my book down and head over to pull a blanket over him. "Goodnight, sleeping beauty," I whisper before heading back to the chair.

I watch whatever is on television until my eyelids become heavy, and I fall into a deep, peaceful sleep.

In the weird maze of my mind, I can't shake this odd desire to make my exit right in the confines of home. Is that too much? To have my folks or my bro stumble upon my lifeless self one day? It's been this ongoing push and pull, with Mom and Dad urging me to set up camp in the hospital, and me just swatting away their plans.

So, they yielded and brought in a hospice nurse. Real talk, it's kind of extra morbid. Dying is this unavoidable thing, right? But hospice, it's like, "Hey, here's the nitty-gritty reality of your situation." And it's heavy.

As the never-ending ticking of the clock keeps rolling, my parents, tired of me resisting the whole hospital scene, wave the white flag and welcome in a hospice nurse. It's like a reminder, a sign that my teenage days are running out. I get the logic, but it's also like having a countdown clock to the end of the show, you know?

This dance with death, once this far-off concept, is suddenly right there, like a nosy neighbor who just won't quit. Hospice, this cold reminder of my imminent fade-out, marks each second like some emotionless metronome, ticking down to the inevitable.

In the middle of this grim tango with my mortality, the vibrant colors of my teenage years start to fade into these muted, melancholic shades of goodbye. The weight of the impending doom, this heavy jacket I can't take off, smothers what's left of my spark. In this sea of bleakness, I'm grappling with the harsh truth that my existence is unraveling, life's threads slipping away like sand through my fingers in an unrelenting hourglass.

Chapter Ten

March

Alright, keeping it real here. I haven't been completely upfront about how things are going. All I want is to live it up before it's lights out, but lately, it feels like I'm stuck in a never-ending snooze fest.

God and I? We're not exactly on speaking terms. You know that whole "God won't give you more than you can handle" line Mom used to drop? Feels more like a cosmic eye roll these days. The past month? It's been me, my room, and a non-stop nap party.

Nurse Lindsay had to get creative with a feeding tube last week. Keeping anything down turned into a mission impossible. I've mastered the art of puking on an empty stomach, a skill I never signed up for. It's like I'm prepping for a crash course in the not-so-glamorous side of six feet under living.

Last night was a rollercoaster, not the fun kind though.

I pulled a solid minute without taking a breath, and in those sixty seconds, I genuinely thought the curtains were closing on this chaotic play called life.

And weirdly, I was okay with it. The idea of bidding farewell to the pain and the struggle felt like catching a break.

But then reality slapped me back into consciousness, and there was Mom, swooping in with the superhero-level timing to slap that oxygen mask on my face.

Don't get me wrong; I love her, but it's like I was one breath away from finally escaping this exhausting game, and she had to go and spoil the moment.

Can't a person catch a break?

I sent out a cosmic plea.

A desperate, whispered wish for an exit ticket from this existence that feels more like a never-ending nightmare. I'm not asking for much, just a gentle slide into the unknown, away from the constant ache and the struggles that make every breath feel like an uphill battle.

I wonder what it's like to be free from this pain, to drift into a peaceful nothingness where oxygen masks and life support are nothing but distant memories, I have forgotten what it's like.

Maybe in that quiet space between breaths, I'd find solace. Maybe there, in the stillness, I'd finally feel weightless, unburdened by the heavy reality of this failing body.

It's not easy to admit, but sometimes I wish for an end to the pain, for a chance to escape this shell of a body that's slowly betraying me. If life's a journey, mine feels like an endless hike up a steep mountain, and I've reached the point where every step is agony. A silent plea echoes through my thoughts, "God, I'm be

Chapter Eleven

April

I throw the idea out there like a lifeline, "How do you feel about taking a little vacation?" I can't help but notice the way Mom hesitates before entering my room. Every spring break, from the time I was in kindergarten to the chaotic days before Kenny's accident, had been a pilgrimage to the beach house. I long to revisit that familiar shore, to feel the grains of sand beneath my fingertips and breathe in the salty ocean air one last time.

"Please, Mom. Please?" My plea is a desperate melody, a chorus of longing that's been building within me for too long. I've mentioned it before, the desire to return to that beach house, but each time, her response has been the same—a silent shake of the head, a dismissal that weighs heavier with each passing day.

Today is different, though.

Today, I'm beyond begging.

Nurse Lindsay, my silent accomplice in this venture, assists me in leaving the confines of my bed. In my wheelchair, I roll my way to the kitchen, where Mom is.

"Dad already agreed," she informs me, her expression stoic. A sigh escapes me, a mix of relief and frustration. "He spoke with the doctors, Lindsay is on board. I want you to come too, and I'm sorry, but we are going with or without you. I just want to go one last time and fill it with a happy memory. I'm sorry."

The weight of my plea hangs in the air, a silent plea for understanding and closure. The beach house holds fragments of my past, a tapestry woven with laughter, love, and the ghostly echoes of a time when life felt infinite. Going back is not just about revisiting a place; it's an attempt to carve a final chapter filled with joy amidst the pages of pain and uncertainty.

Created with Sketch.

"I can't believe this will be our last vacation together." The words slip from my lips, heavy with the weight of impending goodbyes. Mattie, always the voice of reason, shushes me, placing a gentle finger on my lips. "Hey, none of that. This week is going to be great. No cancer talk."

As the sun begins its ascent, painting the sky with hues of pink and gold, we're just about fifteen minutes away from the beach house. A beach sunrise, with its tranquil beauty, unfolds before us. Mom, refusing to join our journey, stands her ground, and I sense a subtle chill in her demeanor toward Dad, as if he's 'siding with' me.

With the beach house on the horizon, I decide to capture the moment, pulling out my phone to snap a quick picture. I sent it to Mom with a simple message:

Wish you were here with us.

May, Dad, and Lindsay take care of the bags, shuttling them inside, while Mattie wheels me toward the beach. The air carries a slight chill, easily remedied by a cozy blanket. Turning to Mattie, I inquire about our plans for the week. "So, what's the agenda?"

"Surprise. Don't try asking because I won't give you even the tiniest hint," he replies, a wide smile gracing his face. We linger on the beach for an hour, watching the waves dance to an unseen rhythm, until a familiar fatigue creeps in, signaling it's time to retreat to the haven of the beach house.

***

Beach house, day three. The sun is playing hide-and-seek with the clouds, and the ocean breeze carries a mixture of serenity and a tinge of longing. I want to immerse myself in the happiness of these moments, but an empty space lingers, a void that only Mom's presence could fill.

Morning attempts to connect with her through calls have been met with rejection, signaling a lingering upset. Dad, sensing the need for a 'daddy-daughter' day, interrupts our movie marathon with a suggestion. "Hey kiddo, why don't we get you dressed and head for lunch?"

With a nonchalant shrug, I agree. "Yeah, give me a few minutes to change out of my pajamas, and I'll be ready." My wheels carry me back to my room, where I shed my nightgown for Lulu shorts, a tank top, and comfy Vans. Grabbing a jacket, I return to the family room, calling out to Dad, only to be met by Mom's unexpected presence.

"Mom!" I exclaim, caught off guard as she envelops me in a heartfelt hug. "I'm sorry for getting upset with you. I should have just been there for you instead of letting my feelings get in the way."

The weight of unspoken emotions lifts, replaced by the warmth of understanding. We share a meaningful conversation before Dad joins us, and together, we head to my favorite diner for a heartfelt lunch.

As night falls, we transform into our pajamas, creating a cozy scene with popcorn and a movie. The day's events have taken their toll on Mattie, whose head finds a comfortable spot in my lap, serenaded by the soothing sounds of his snoring.

***

Today marks the end of our beach house retreat, the final sun-kissed day in this cherished haven. Mom, seizing the moment, surprised me with rose bushes, a symbolic gesture to embed our memories into the very soil of this property. She hinted at future visits, ensuring the beach house remains a part of our lives.

The day unfolded, and by noon, the air buzzed with peculiar vibes. Mom and May exchanged cryptic glances, and Mattie and Paxton vanished into the mysterious abyss. We resumed our floral project around six, though my contribution lagged behind due to frequent breaks to accommodate my energy levels.

Lunch came and went, filled with a blend of laughter and unspoken sentiments. Mom and May worked tirelessly, creating a floral tapestry around our temporary sanctuary. Lindsay, ever-supportive, assisted me with a refreshing bath, while Mom undertook the mission of tidying up. It felt like an eternity, especially the meticulous effort to rid my nails of persistent dirt.

Upon returning to my room, a neatly bowed box and a note awaited me, a signature move only Mattie could execute with such finesse.

> *Its prom night! Put this on and meet me in the main room.*
>
> *-Mattie*

In that intimate moment, as I opened the box and revealed the exquisite satin emerald green prom dress, the world seemed to pause. The delicate fabric whispered promises of a night transcending the boundaries of our reality.

"Oh, Mattie," I breathed, my heart swelling with gratitude and love. Lindsay's deft hands transformed me, adorning me in the dress that spoke of Mattie's care and affection. With each delicate touch, a silent symphony of emotions played out in the room.

As I wheeled into the main hall, Mattie's voice, soft as a secret, reached my ear. "You look stunning, Addie," he murmured. A kiss on my cheek carried the weight of a thousand unspoken words, leaving me breathless.

Our parents, capturing the essence of this ephemeral beauty, surrounded us with the click of cameras. The images etched in time, a testament to a night we would carry with us into the unknown.

Led by Mattie, I ventured to the back patio, where an enchanting scene unfolded. Soft beams adorned with fairy lights crisscrossed the sky, and the pool shimmered with lotus lights and the flicker of candles. A table, adorned with a curated menu, whispered of meticulous planning and an unwavering love.

My eyes welled with tears, witnessing the culmination of Mattie's efforts and the embodiment of a love that defied the harsh reality we faced.

Amidst the enchanting ambiance, Mattie and I shared a dinner infused with laughter, tears, and the silent acknowledgment of the limited time we had left. The strains of Kodaline's acoustic "Love Like This" serenaded us as Mattie rose, extending his hand for the dance that awaited.

"I know you didn't want cancer talk this week, but, Mattie, I need you to know how thankful I am to have had you through all of this," I confessed as he wiped away my tears.

"Addie, life has been so unfair to you, but don't doubt the love I have for you," he assured me, the weight of his words echoing in the quiet night.

"I love you too, Mattie, us against the world," I whispered with a trembling smile.

"No, Addley. I love you. I'm pretty sure I have been in love with you since forever," he declared, his words mingling with the soft melody that surrounded us.

As I attempted to respond, my voice caught in my throat, and all I could do was bawl into his chest, soaking in the overwhelming emotion that bound us together.

"Believe me when I say this," Mattie continued, locking eyes with mine, "When someone asks about my first lover, I'm going to tell them about you and how you made me feel because that is the strongest love I have ever and will ever hold for someone. I love you so much it hurts, Addley Rose McRae."

In that poignant confession, time stood still, and our love became a timeless symphony, echoing through the corridors of our shared existence.

Chapter Twelve

May

On the fateful night of May 20, Addley Rose McRae's journey on this mortal coil concluded, leaving behind a world draped in the shadows of sorrow. The quiet hum of existence seemed to hush, as if nature itself held its breath in acknowledgment of an irreversible departure.

In the hallowed silence, a subtle thump echoed through the room, an unwitting herald of the impending tragedy. Mrs. McRae, a devoted guardian, rushed to her daughter's side, only to witness the heart-wrenching descent from the desk chair. Addley, fragile and ethereal, gasped for air, her plea for liberation stifled by the grasp of an invisible force.

"Please let me go," Addley's plea resonated, a poignant whisper that seemed to linger in the room long after her voice had faded. Mrs. McRae, in a mother's instinctual embrace, cradled her daughter's limp form, caught between the realms of hope and an unavoidable farewell.

As the ambulance carried Addley away, the blinking red and white lights painted the night in hues of inevitability. The hospital, a beacon of both healing and sorrow, became the stage for the final act in Addley's ephemeral drama.

Within the sterile confines of the hospital room, the gravity of the moment settled. Medical professionals, their expressions etched with empathy, treaded lightly through the delicate dance between life and its inevitable counterpart.

In a room bathed in the sterile glow of hospital lights, the universe made its declaration. At precisely nine forty-two, Addley Rose McRae, a soul too young to embrace the full spectrum of life, departed, leaving behind an indelible imprint on the hearts of those who had shared in her journey. The silent tears of Mrs. McRae bore witness to the ephemeral nature of existence, a truth that, even in its profound sadness, held a poignant beauty.

Chapter Thirteen

Epilogue

In the dim glow of the bookstore, I delicately close Addley's diary, setting it down beside the book adorned with her radiant picture. The weight of the years hangs in the air as I take a moment to absorb the gravity of what I'm about to share with the world. The diary, a testament to Addley's indomitable spirit, holds the chronicles of her final year – a poignant journey etched in ink, immortalizing her dreams, struggles, and the enduring light she emanated even on her darkest days.

Addley's departure a week before graduation shattered the illusion of invincibility, leaving a void that time could never fully heal. The collective shock, anger, and confusion reverberated through the community, questioning the capricious nature of fate that could snatch away someone so perfect and seemingly untouched by mortality.

Her mom entrusted me with the diary, a sacred responsibility that carried Addley's final words and aspirations. The note within it spoke volumes, a silent plea for me to share her story with the world. Today marks the fruition of that promise – "Love Always, Addley" is now out in the world, a literary testament to a life that burned brightly against the encroaching shadows of illness.

Standing before the eager faces filling the bookstore, I clear my throat, preparing to speak words that have waited five long years to escape. The crowd, stretching beyond the confines of the store, reflects the enduring impact of Addley's life. I hold up her book, a tangible relic of her spirit, and begin my heartfelt proclamation.

"This book is more than words on paper; it's the narrative of the most incredible person I ever had the privilege of calling my best friend and first love. Addley McRae, though cancer claimed her, lives on through these pages. May you all come to cherish her as deeply as I do."

As I reclaim my seat, a crumpled piece of paper emerges from my pocket – a list of dreams, plans, and accomplishments that Addley and I had scribbled down together. With a pen in hand, I ceremoniously mark off the final accomplishment, a bittersweet testament to a promise fulfilled and a love that endures beyond the constraints of time.

Chapter Fourteen

Epilogue Reimagined

<u>This is a reimagined ending; a version where Addie chose to fight and overcame her diagnosis.</u>

***

Five years later, I flip through the pages of my old diary, my fingers lingering on the edges of my handwriting. It feels surreal, reading the words of a girl who once thought she might not have a future. But here I am, alive and thriving, my picture smiling back at me from the cover of my book, "Love Always, Addley."

My decision to fight cancer was the hardest choice I ever made, but it was also the best. Against all odds, I survived.

Graduation day was a triumph, not just for me, but for everyone who supported me through my journey. Walking across that stage, feeling the applause and love from my family and friends, I knew I had made it.

I went on to college, majoring in creative writing, determined to share my story and inspire others. Volunteering at hospitals became my passion. Talking to kids who were going through what I had endured gave me purpose. Seeing their eyes light up with hope made every struggle worth it.

My book, "Love Always, Addley," became a bestseller. It's filled with my raw, honest experiences —my fears, my pain, and most importantly, my unwavering hope. Letters from readers all over the world poured in, telling me how my story has touched their lives and given them the courage to face their own battles.

Today, as I stand at the podium in a packed bookstore, I feel an overwhelming sense of pride and gratitude. The line of people waiting to meet me wraps around the block. It's not just about my story anymore; it's about the hope and resilience that it represents.

"Thank you all for coming," I begin, my voice steady but emotional. "This book is more than just a story. It's a testament to the strength and resilience we all have inside us. Five years ago, I was scared and unsure of what the future held. But with the love of my family, friends, and all of you, I found the strength to keep going. This book is for anyone who has ever felt lost or afraid. It's a reminder that no matter how dark things get, there is always hope."

As I finish speaking, I glance over at Mattie, my rock through all of this. He's been there every step of the way, and I couldn't have done it without him. We share a smile, and I can see the pride in his eyes.

We sit down to sign copies of my book, and Mattie pulls out a crumpled piece of paper. It's his bucket list, and with a smile, he crosses off the final item: "Help Addley achieve her dreams."

He hands the paper to me, and as I read it, my eyes fill with tears. "We did it, Mattie," I whisper, hugging him tightly.

In that moment, I know this is just the beginning. Together, we'll continue to inspire and give hope to others, sharing our story and living life to the fullest. Because if there's one thing I've learned, it's that every day is a gift, and with love and determination, we can overcome anything.

Later that night, after the book signing, we gather with our closest friends and family. There's laughter, stories, and so much love in the room. I look around and realize how far I've come from the girl who once thought she might not have a future. Now, I'm living my dream, surrounded by the people I love.

As the evening winds down, Mattie takes my hand and leads me outside. The night is cool, and the stars are bright above us. "I have something for you," he says, pulling out a small box. Inside is a necklace with a delicate charm that reads "Hope."

"It's a reminder," he says softly, "that no matter what happens, there's always hope."

I hug him tightly, my heart full. "Thank you, Mattie. For everything."

He smiles, and we stand there for a while, just holding each other, looking up at the stars. In that moment, I feel a deep sense of peace and gratitude. Life hasn't been easy, but it's been beautiful in its own way.

Mattie pulls back slightly, still holding my hands. His eyes are serious now, filled with a depth of emotion that makes my heart skip a beat. "Addley, there's something else," he says, his voice barely above a whisper.

Before I can respond, he gets down on one knee and opens another small box. Inside is the most beautiful ring I have ever seen. My breath catches in my throat, tears instantly springing to my eyes.

"Addley Rose McRae, you are my best friend, my first love, and my forever. Will you marry me?" His voice trembles slightly, but his eyes are steady, filled with love and hope.

For a moment, I can't speak. My mind races through every memory, every struggle, every triumph we've shared. I think about how he's been my rock, my constant, through everything. And in this moment, I know with absolute certainty what my answer is.

"Yes, Mattie," I whisper, tears streaming down my face. "Yes, of course I'll marry you."

He slips the ring onto my finger, and as he stands, he pulls me into the tightest hug. We both laugh through our tears, overwhelmed by the joy and love we feel.

Our friends and family, who had been watching from a distance, erupt into cheers and applause. As we turn to face them, I feel an overwhelming sense of gratitude. For the love we've shared, for the future we're about to build, and for the hope that has carried us through the darkest times.

As we lie together under the stars, I hold Mattie's hand and look at the ring on my finger. I think about the journey we've been on, and the incredible future that lies ahead. And I know, without a doubt, that with Mattie by my side, I can face anything.

Because love, in all its forms, is the greatest gift of all.

And our love story, with all its twists and turns, is just beginning.

The End

Biographical note

Brittany Anne discovered her passion for storytelling at a young age and began writing as a form of self-expression. Although she started her writing journey earlier in life, it was only after a profound family tragedy that she decided to share her work with the world. Her debut novel, "Twelve Months," is a poignant coming-of-age tale in the young adult genre.

Motivated by personal experiences, Brittany Anne's storytelling is a reflection of the complexities of growing up, loss, and the indomitable spirit of youth.

"Twelve Months" explores the depths of sorrow and the transformative power of time, capturing the raw emotions of its characters.

Brittany, now a dedicated stay-at-home mom, brings a unique perspective to her writing—a blend of youthful creativity and wisdom from navigating life's challenges. While "Twelve Months" marks her debut in the literary world, Brittany Anne's ability to evoke empathy and convey profound emotions positions her as a promising voice in young adult fiction.

Connect with Brittany Anne and stay updated on her writing journey by visiting her facebook page: **Brittany Anne Author**